FOR NO GOOD REASON

Steve Banko

NFB

Buffalo, New York

Cover Painting by Marleah Doherty

NFB
<<<>>>
No Frills Buffalo/Amelia Press
119 Dorchester Road
Buffalo, New York 14213

For more information visit

nfbpublishing.com

DEDICATION

To John and Shirley ... without John, there would be no Shirley; without Shirley, there would be no me.

This book is also dedicated to the Garryowen troopers of Company D, 2nd Battalion, 7th U.S. Cavalry who fought and bled and died under the aegis of the 1st Cavalry Division on 3 December 1968.

It is also dedicated to my wife and to all the wives, spouses, girlfriends, mothers and fathers, and friends of those who served and continue to serve our nation with honor and courage. I have always felt that should someone wish to hear a war story they should talk to those who waited for us to return only to be the targets of all the anger, pain, and frustration that is so much a part of combat service. Without them, there would be no "us."

For No Good Reason

"Dulce et decorum est, pro patria mori."

- Horace

"In the old days, they wrote that is was sweet and fitting
to die for one's country.
In modern war, there's nothing sweet nor fitting.
You die like a dog for no good reason."

- Ernest Hemingway, Notes on the Next War

PROLOGUE

I didn't get my ticket to hell punched in any of the glamorous ways. I'd spent so much of my young life wrapped up in the superstitions of my religion that I didn't have time or courage enough to do something juicy. My itinerary didn't include the battering (or even the denting) of Commandments five, six, seven, or eight. I was too busy earning special bonus points to get me to heaven to even think that a layover in Purgatory would be on my Trip-Tik. My route didn't include any of the commandments at all. I got to go to hell because I failed ROTC. No kidding: a half-credit course and everyone's panties were in a bunch

Really. That was the big crime. I didn't screw anybody's wife. I didn't steal anything. I didn't kill anyone. I hadn't blasphemed. I didn't skip Mass. Hell, I served Mass for the big guy—the bishop himself, miter, crosier and all. I didn't even have hair on the palms of my hands.

I just decided I didn't like to dress up like some latter-day Boy Scout and march all over the athletic field three times a week. That was my big crime—the one that got me assigned among the damned.

My name is Josh Duffy: Joshua Jeremiah Duffy, actually. My parents couldn't decide which biblical prophet would be my patron. I understand the debate raged for hours and when mother won out with the hero of the Old Testament, Pa got drunk for four days and nights in protest. Truth be told though, the old man would have gotten drunk for five days and nights in celebration had he won. But you get the picture. With a moniker like that I almost had "priest" stenciled on my forehead at my baptism. So I had kids in the playground call me Josh. Punishment for calling me Joshua was an ass whipping so bad the offender would catch another one from his old man just for getting his ass kicked so badly. Mother always thought that I would become God's avenging angel, although you can bet her genuine imitation crystal rosary beads from the Vatican that she never thought her wish would come true the way it did.

Either you've already assumed that I would be educated in Catholic schools or your name is Shlomo. I did OK through most of it, jocking it up in every season and getting good marks. It wasn't until I went away to college that things started to turn down a path I didn't expect. Away

from home for the first time in my life, going to school
with girls, being old enough to drink all ganged up on me
at the same time. Then throw in Reserve Officer Training
Corps—Rot-see for short—and my doom was predictable as
my Saturday morning hangover. Did I forget to mention that
my father gave me more than that unsightly fur that crawled
down my back? He gave me that dear fondness for the drink
and, oh, how I cultivated it.

As you can imagine then, it would be redundant
to say that I was hung over like a moose on the day I got
summoned to the office of the Dean of Admissions. I tried to
put on my best face for the meeting but my unsteady hand
tore it to shreds on the end of a Gillette Adjustable™. I was
trying to simplify my life and they come up with a razor with
nine settings. I entered the Dean's office with all those little
pieces of toilet paper hanging off me like a bad float in the
Rose Parade. I knew things were headed down the wrong
path when I smiled and gave the dean a big hello and in
return, he offered me a Tic-Tac. When I started to shake one
out of the plastic box, he told me to keep them.

Then he got right to the point.

"You screwed up big time, Mr. Duffy," he said, trying
not to get down wind of me. "Take a good look around the
campus when you leave. It will be your last."

I searched through my addled brain to try to imagine

what egregious offense I'd committed that would send me home in shame but it was no use.

"What did I do?" I asked, cleverly.

"It's what you didn't do, Duffy. You failed ROTC."

I started to laugh but stopped when I noticed I was laughing alone.

"You're kidding, right?" I said. "ROTC's only half a credit. I might make the Dean's List this semester, even with a ROTC 'F'."

The dean had been holding two copies of the college handbook. Both were bookmarked. He opened one and handed the other to me. He looked down his ample nose into the lens of his glasses until he found the passage he was looking for. My book was already highlighted.

"Read with me, if you will, my good man... 'all male undergraduate students are required to successfully complete four semesters of Military Science. Those semesters will be completed during the freshman and sophomore years. After the basic course, male students may elect to continue in Military Science studies leading to a commission in the Field Artillery branch of the United States Army.' "

I was still confused.

"So I failed ROTC," I allowed. "What's the big deal? I didn't know you guys took this stuff so seriously. I'll make it up, OK?"

"You don't read any better than you listen, Duffy," the dean said. "The commander of the program has terminated you. You can't make up anything because he has declared you persona non grata. He said he's going to make you an example for all the hippies who don't take ROTC seriously."

Hippie? I wondered. I wear khaki pants and Adler socks. Where the hell is that coming from?

The dean took off his glasses and looked me in the eye.

"You didn't follow instructions regarding Military Science and now you can't meet the course requirement because the commander won't let you back into the program. Is this getting any clearer?"

This sounded like bullshit to me.

"With all due respect, this doesn't seem exactly fair. Kick me out of school for failing theology but not because I don't like looking like a Boy Scout and marching all over the soccer field."

I thought I won some big points with the theology thing. I was wrong.

"Well, well, well, Mr. Duffy, you are now setting the rules for the university. I feel almost moved to apologize for asking you to abide by our rules when yours are so much more to your liking. But every now and then I am forced to think about what your arrogance and your disdain for our rules costs this university and I wonder why we let you in this institution in the first place. I wouldn't expect you to know this, Duffy, but we receive much needed federal aid to this school based on the number of men who successfully complete the basic ROTC course. We need that money, Duffy—desperately! Now, we won't get it because you think yourself too suave and debonair to wear the uniform of your country and march an hour a week."

"But..."

"I am not finished, Duffy! Now it's our turn, Mr. Suave and Debonair. It's our turn to enforce the rules we lay down for this university."

Now I got it and getting it meant realizing I was in deep do-do. None of this was about rules or failing or anything. It was about money. I screwed with the bottom line and that was something you didn't do to a Catholic college. Why couldn't they just have done the Christian thing and had bingo instead of ROTC? I threw myself on the mercy of a merciful dean.

"I worked summers in the mills to save money for this tuition. I am not getting any help from my parents. I am paying my own way here. You know what happens if I get kicked out of here: I get drafted. It's that simple. Can't you cut me a little slack here?"

I think I got to the old man a little. His position softened ever so slightly.

"I thought of that, Duffy. That's why I called the commandant and asked him to reserve decision until he met with you. He's agreed. You convince him to let you back into the ROTC program and you can stay. He's waiting for you in his office right now."

I'd spent a lifetime not being intimidated by bigger, stronger jocks. I'd faced up to and faced down a lot of guys who thought they were tough. Growing up Irish in an 'Eye-talian' neighborhood makes that mandatory. But none of that macho stuff, none of that mine's-bigger-than-yours bullshit, none of the swagger I'd adopted since winning the drinking contest at Booty's Hotel—none of it was working for me as I made my way across campus to plead my case to the ROTC commandant. I had that churning in the pit of the stomach you feel you know you really screwed up and now it was time to pay. It was a feeling I got when I'd beat the shit out of my kid brother on the playground. I was a tough guy on the street but when my brother took off bawling for home, I realized the toughest guy I knew would be waiting for me with his belt already out of his pants. The walk home never took nearly as long as I wanted it to. Neither did the walk to Quonset hut where the commandant had his office.

I got a bad feeling as soon as I walked into the place.

It was more like a crypt than an office. I recognized the guy sitting behind the desk as one of my drinking buddies but as much as I knew his face I had no idea what his name was. The crypt was decorated with a bunch of military shit like rifles and helmets and cannon shells. One whole wall was plastered with pictures that looked like they were taken during the Civil War. I got the itchy feeling the commandant had been in the army with Ulysses S. Grant.

I put on a confident face for my friend behind the desk, all the while feeling an impending sense of doom.

"Hey! My man, how you doing? I'm here to see the commandant."

"I know, Duff. He's waiting for you. Be real cool in there. He can be a real asshole when he wants to be."

Why did I not need to be told that?

He opened the door to the inner sanctum and I could barely see this little head peeking over the top of the desk. Two small hands were folded in front of the little head. I honest-to-God knew I was doing something I would regret but I walked in anyway. As I was approaching the desk, I saw a picture behind the little guy. It was yellow and cracking, like the old man's head. The guy in the picture was standing next to a horse drawn cannon. When I finally got a gander at the old man, he reminded me of a raisin: all brown and wrinkled.

"Ah, sir, the dean suggested I come and talk..."

"Stand at attention when you are addressing a superior officer!"

The old guy had a voice that wasn't cracking. I expected to see Toto in the corner with a curtain in his mouth. Time to regroup.

"Right, sir... I was..."

"You are at attention, troop! You speak when I tell you to speak!"

Now I knew why my stomach was churning like a flushing toilet. The old guy knew he had me by the short hairs and he started pulling.

"I know why you are here, Mr. Duffy. You have come crawling to my office to beg your way back into my program. You are facing rightful dismissal from this university because you made the mistake of thinking yourself too good for the Army."

"Well, not exactly sir. You see..."

"Shut up! That's exactly why you are here! I know a lot more about you than you might think, Mr. Duffy, and the more I know, the more I despise. You are one of those despicable punks who inflict yourself on respectable schools like this only to act like a common hooligan, drinking and chasing women. You..."

Now it was my turn to interrupt. I was losing but I

wasn't going down without get my licks in.

"If you think I came here for the coeds, old man, you need corneal transplants."

"That's enough, Duffy! You will only respond to direct questions. Your smart remarks and childish attempts at humor do not impress or interest me! I've seen a hundred like you, a thousand perhaps. You are all blather and bull crap. You refuse regimentation. You reject discipline. You are unruly and uncontrollable. That's why you shrink from military life. You are an undisciplined wastrel who will be a vagrant all your life."

This guy was really hitting below the belt. Me, a wastrel? (whatever that meant) The more this guy talked, the better he sounded to himself and the more he laid it on. Time to get mine in again.

"Old man, you don't know shit. I never even went to your silly class, remember? So take your foolish army and stick it..."

The geezer slammed a swagger stick down on the desk with a loud bang. He was really losing it now.

"I'm not wasting any more time with you, Duffy. You are a punk, a common lout. You will never amount to anything because you lack the basic human element of discipline. You are destined to be a drunk and a slacker. You are not only to be expelled from this school but you will be drafted at once. You will be drafted because I've already called your draft board to tell them the circumstances of your dismissal. You will be sent to Vietnam, Duffy. That's where they send all the screw-ups. And because you lack the discipline it takes to be a real soldier you will screw up and get yourself killed just like all the other duds and drop-outs."

The raisin man was talking very fast now, getting more excited as he got closer to the part where I was going to die. His wrinkles flushed from the craggy brown to a bright red and I thought he might go into cardiac arrest. But I couldn't even catch that break. The old bastard slowed down and as he did, I knew my ticket to hell had just been issued. This was worse than when my old man gave me a whipping. At least, there was an end to those. I had the awful feeling that this ass kicking was going to go on for a long time.

CHAPTER ONE

WELCOME TO THE 'NAM

Most people subscribe to the popular myth that the evildoers go to hell after they die. I don't believe that all despite all the *Baltimore Catechism* drilled into me on the flat side of a nun wielded ruler. Hell is for the living. That way you can feel all the pain. You can be overwhelmed by despair so intense you can feel it sucking the dreams from your head and the spirit from your soul. That's the kind of hell I was feeling when the driver of that jeep sped off shifting his gears, leaving me alone with my fear on the side of the road.

The heat was something otherworldly. This sun didn't shine. It glared. I didn't see any clouds in the sky that day, but I can't be sure because I couldn't see any sky. There was just this molten, colorless mass up there, as though the sun was melting the sky. It sure as hell was melting me. I was expecting a tangled mass of foreboding jungle when I came to Vietnam but now I was looking across a bleak, sun-bleached landscape that was as empty as I felt. Only the khaki-colored dust kicked up by the jeep moved. I stretched a little, just to put some motion into the picture and tried to work some of the stiffness out of my back.

I was standing in front of the same sort of building I'd encountered since stepping onto Vietnamese soil two days ago: four walls of dust-covered screen surrounding a concrete slab and covered by a corrugated tin roof. The dusty sign over the door identified the hut as the Home of the Recon Platoon. Someone had scrawled seven words in Magic Marker beneath the official lettering. They read: Find 'em. Fix 'em. Fuck 'em up. Nice and simple, I thought. I can remember that. When I felt the sweat running down my spine and into the crack of my ass, I decided it was time to enter my new home. I slung the M-16 over my shoulder and hoisted my duffel bag and walked in.

When my eyes finally adjusted from the white-hot sunlight to the darkness of the hut, I was shocked by what I saw. The place looked like the office of the scurvy-assed junkyard at the end of my street; except this junkyard was strewn with every kind of weapon I'd ever even seen and a few I had never seen. I thought maybe the Viet Cong had sneaked into the place and killed the bodies I saw laying in full dress on cots all over the dark room. The only evidence they were alive was the hideous noises that growled out of them from time to time.

The air inside the place was close and hot and stunk of sweat. It was littered with belts of machine gun ammo, hand grenades, claymore mines, knives, and guns. Loaded rifle magazines were scattered across the concrete the way a child's blocks might litter a nursery. Canteens, ammo cans, empty food containers and a few machetes were included in the array. This was my first indication that the stateside army rules might not be fully enforced here. I tiptoed through the mess, half not wanting to wake anyone and half not wanting to contaminate myself with whatever disease might have infected this place. As I moved deeper into the pit, I was drawn to a scraping noise coming from the back of the hut. As I got closer to the noise, I could make out the shape of a guy sitting near the screen door in back. I closed in, expecting to see some peg-legged long hair with an eye-patch and a parrot on his shoulder. Instead, I saw a scruffy looking guy running a thick-bladed hunting knife back and forth across a sharpening stone.

Jesus, I whispered to myself, as I moved in closer, could these guys really be soldiers? Can they actually be our soldiers?

The guy sat there, stroking the blade, entranced by the grating noise it made. He was dressed in filthy fatigue pants, faded from olive drab to merely drab. His feet were bare except for some dirty shower flip-flops that did nothing to hide several raw, oozing sores. His stare was vacant, his eyes unfocused. His faced had been ravaged by something, probably the same purple-red crud now eating his feet. His hair might have been blonde once but today it was dusty gray. His hands manipulated the knife skillfully, as though it was an extension of his fingers. He completed another dozen strokes before he noticed me.

"Hey dude! Where'd you come from?"

"Pennsylvania," I heard my mouth say, knowing that wasn't the answer. "My name's Duffy - Josh Duffy. I'm supposed to report to the Recon Platoon. Am I in the right place?"

"Troop, this here is the 'Nam and ain't nobody ever called this shit-hole the right place. But you found Recon all right. You got any stateside groceries in that duffel bag, Troop?"

Groceries? I thought. Did I miss the Food King on the way in?

"Oh... you mean food. No man, we ate all I had back at Division."

This conversation was going nowhere. I changed the

subject.

"Am I supposed to report to someone?"

"Yeah, probably," my new friend allowed. "But the guys were out on a bush last night, you know?"

It was my turn to look vacant and when I did, he knew that I didn't know.

"Ambush, you F-N-G."

"Oh yeah, sure. Ambush. Gotcha." I didn't think there was anything to lose by playing along.

"Lookie here, Duffy. I wouldn't advise you waking anybody up just yet, especially not for something dumb-assed like reporting. Ain't nobody going to cotton to that shit.

"Besides...

My new friend was obviously on a roll.

"What are they gonna do if you report late? Send your green ass to Viet-fucking-Nam?"

The scurvy soldier laughed loudly at his little bon mot but I didn't see the humor.

"Anybody mind if a real grunt gets a little fucking sleep, gentlemen?"

Ah, I thought, another voice heard from. This might be a good thing. I looked in the direction of the sound and watched a pile of dirty camouflage stir before it finally revealed a shiny black mane and an unshaven face.

"Sorry, amigo," scurvy man said quietly. "Just briefing the FNG here. We'll take it outside, OK?"

I wondered when I became an FNG. I also wondered what an FNG was.

"Fuck you," the talking bundle of rags said. "Who the fuck are you to be briefing anybody? Last time you saw action it was your hand in your pants."

Now that, I thought, was funny.

"What the fuck are you laughing at, FNG?" he said.

There's that term again, I thought.

"What's an FNG?" I asked both of them.

"It's you," my newest friend said. "You—a fucking new guy. An F-N-G."

I didn't know if I should be insulted, but looking at the vast array of weapons within easy reach of the amigo, I felt I could let it slide.

A bare, brown torso festooned with tattoos joined the black head of hair peeking from the blankets.

"The Mexican is the best fucking point man in Vietnam," scurvy man told me, with obvious awe.

"Point man" was a term I had heard frequently in infantry training. It was spoken with as much awe back in the States as it was here.

"I'm Duffy," I said extending my hand. "Glad to know you."

He ignored it.

"You got any food, gringo?"

"Naw, he's clean," the scurvy guy said, beating me to the punch.

"No food? What the fuck good are you?" the point man asked me.

Damn, first day and I'm stumped for answers, I thought.

"What's going on back in the World? Those fucking college kids still marching and chanting and shit?"

I couldn't imagine either of these two guys in my world back home so I ignored the question. The point man didn't mind.

"Now that you two jerk-offs woke me up, what you got planned for entertainment?"

I was really stumped now. Little, short of human sacrifice, could have entertained this guy.

"The FNG don't got no chow but I bet he's got some cash," the scurvy man said. "Maybe he could souvenir us a little hum and cum at the Number One."

I looked to point man for translation.

"He's horny. That's like saying the sun is hot. He wants you to buy us a piece of ass as the Number One Laundry."

The translation was only adding to my confusion.

"You go to the Laundromat to fuck?" I asked.

"No fuckhead," the point man said. "The laundry is in the front. The whores are in the back."

"And the hum and cum?" I added, not really wanting to know the answer.

"He wants a blow job."

Silly me. It was all as plain as day now.

The point man stood and revealed that he slept in pants and combat boots. The lion tattooed on his right breast flexed as he opened the back door.

"There's the Senora Momma-san's little pleasure palace," he said with the awe I was reserving for point men. I looked where he was pointing and saw nothing. Maybe these guys had imaginary whores.

Scurvy took my head and twisted it in the right direction. A little shack sat across a flat brown plain, glistening in the blistering sun.

"What's shining like that?" I asked. "They got silver paint or something?"

¡Ay, *caramba!* " The fucking walls are made from flattened beer and soda cans."

Silly me--again.

"That little shack is a laundry and a whorehouse?"

"Hey, FNG, you gotta make do with what you got. You dig?"

The scurvy guy chimed in.

"And you gotta admit, Duffy, a warm whore is a damn sight better than Rosie Palm," he said laughing loudly.

I do? I wondered.

The point man punched the dirty man hard on the arm.

"Knock it off, you rotten-footed asshole. The guys are sleeping."

I thought the point guy was showing admirable concern for the other members of the platoon but he ruined the moment.

"Besides, I doubt the FNG can buy a whole platoon a piece of pussy."

Then he turned to me and asked: "How much cash you got, FNG?"

"I think I got sixty dollars left."

The smile showed shining teeth that whitened the point man's deep brown face. Two other things came to mind: this guy had serious designs on my cash and I'd never been to a whorehouse in my life. Whorehouse? I'd never been laid in my life. All that Catholic upbringing had left me reasonably convinced that the first time I'd have sex outside of wedlock, I'd have a heart attack and die, going straight to hell. Now, I'd taken the express to hell without making any of the fun stops. Maybe dying would be a desired alternative to this place. What the fuck? I reasoned. How bad could actually getting laid be? Still, who the fuck were these guys to be spending my money?

The point man stood. He pointed with a bayonet to a frameless face pinned to the wall near his bunk.

"My woman," he said proudly. Then he picked a dirty towel off the floor and threw it on the nail, covering the picture. "She'd probably understand but what she don't know won't hurt her, right?"

Hell no, I said to myself, but the double dose of clap and syphilis you could give her might.

The scurvy man grabbed a helmet and a rifle and threw on a shirt. He didn't bother to button it or tuck it into his pants.

Then we stepped into the fevered shimmer of the dry season sun and headed toward the perimeter wire about five hundred meters away.

"Whoa," I said. "The gate is over that way. I was told we couldn't legally leave the base except through the gate."

"*Madre Dios*, gringo," the point man growled, pointing at the scurvy guy. "The trick word is 'legal.' We'd have a problem explaining his uniform, no?"

Scurvy looked as much like a soldier as he did a Harlem Globetrotter.

"You could be right," I said. Even an FNG knows

things.

We walked on at a quick pace and when we reached the first strand of barbed wire, the point man stopped us with a raised hand. Scurvy took the lead.

"This man's dick is like a divining rod," the Mexican said. "You follow every footstep he takes, no matter what. You got that? You just walk where he walks."

"How come?" I asked.

"Never fucking mind 'how come?' You just do it, you understand?"

"Yeah, but..."

"No fucking 'buts'. Just fucking listen!"

I didn't think I liked the Mexican anymore, point man or not. Who the fuck did he think he was messing with here?

If I was concerned that the point man wasn't walking point on our little trek, I kept it to myself. The scurvy guy started out slowly, in a crazy weave that made us walk over a hundred meters to cover about twenty meters of wire. I grew more skeptical with every step—convinced my new buddies were jerking me around. I also grew a lot more apprehensive. I told myself our unauthorized walk was at the heart of the gnawing chewing in my stomach and was on its way to my heart.

But I wasn't that good a liar.

For twenty-one years I treated this thing called

virginity like it was something worth saving. Religion was huge to me. My father used to tell me that each human action triggered a reaction somewhere in God's universe and that the universe was long retribution but much less expansive with compassion or understanding. The God of my father might have compassion for wanting to, but I couldn't really see Him forgiving me for actually doing it.

"*New Guy!*"

The Mexican's shout snapped me back from the come and gone to the here and now.

"I told you to follow the leader. You aren't doing that. Get your head out of your ass and do what you're told!"

I'd drifted a few feet to the left of the track left by scurvy's shower shoes.

What's the big deal, I thought. In the real world this guy would be picking peaches but here he wants to tell me what to do. Still, I moved back into the groove and followed the leader.

We were crossing a series of six barbed wire obstacles that covered about 150 straight-line meters but we had to have walked at least ten times that far, weaving in and around the wire. What I thought would have been a ten-minute walk was now approaching twenty minutes. As we neared the last row of stacked concertina wire, the sweat that soaked me plastered my shirt to my skin. Scurvy was sweating too but not like me. The Mexican looked amazingly fresh.

"Christ, look at me," I blurted out. "I can't see any chicks looking like this."

My mouth was talking appearance but my brain was thinking fear. The whorehouse was looming pretty large on my ethical horizon. The numbing fear that I didn't even know how to fuck was becoming a big factor in my deciding this whorehouse thing might not be a great idea after all.

Of course, my two new "friends" heard only my mouth. I could already guess how they would respond and I wasn't disappointed. They mocked the shit out of me.

Mex grabbed his crotch and flashed those incredibly white teeth again.

"Shee-it, Duffy, Momma-san don't care what your clothes look like. She wants to know how your pesos jingle. 'Sides, you weren't no GQ model when your clothes were dry."

The scurvy man must have felt obliged to follow suit.

"If looks was hand grenades, new guy, you wouldn't have enough to blow your nose."

That was a little more than I felt even an FNG should have to take. Here was the captain of the ugly team making fun of me.

"Christ, if you fuck like you walk, I might not have

enough money for the three of us," I joked.

Scurvy got a stupid looking, shit-eating grin on his face, and I started to wonder if the serpentine walk through the barbed wire was some sort of stupid hazing.

"What was that little game back there in the barbed wire? Vietnam's version of freshman initiation?"

The Mexican started to answer but Scurvy interrupted him.

"Fuck no, newbie. That wasn't no initiation. Unless you call walking through a minefield 'initiation.'"

I shot a look at the amigo and knew the ugly guy wasn't bullshitting. My knees felt like water and my stomach starting churning. The headline "Local GI Killed While Entering Whorehouse" flashed through my mind. The rage that anyone would take my life this lightly needed addressing. I grabbed the shorter Mexican by the shirt with both hands, pulling him up to my height.

"Why didn't you tell me, you little cocksucker?" I growled.

The Mexican dropped his weapon and broke my hold on him with an upward thrust of his forearms. His hands reached behind my head and yanked it forward at the same time he shot his forehead at me like a weapon. I twisted just enough to catch the blow intended for my nose with my cheekbone. The explosive blow started my eye swelling like a fresh blown balloon. Even as it swelled, I grabbed a handful of the Mexican's balls and started to squeeze. His mouth opened in a silent scream and he let go of my head.

"I'm new here, you greaser prick," I said, "but I ain't newly born. Don't fuck with me, beaner. Don't fuck with me." I kept one eye on scurvy man but the sudden violence had paralyzed him.

"Let go of me," the Mexican said. "Let go of me right now and I won't kill you the first chance I get."

That sounded reasonable. I made my point, even though it would look like the Mexican got the best of me. Furthermore, I believed he would try to kill me. I let him go.

"Now what about the minefield?" I asked. "Why the fuck didn't you tell me?"

"It don't mean anything, FNG. You were in good hands. This rotten-footed prick knows more about this minefield than anybody does. Ain't that right, buddy?"

"Fucking-A, man! I laid this minefield," Scurvy beamed. "Come to think of it, I laid everything else in and around this village too."

Despite my anger, I couldn't help but laugh at the thought of this leper-looking idiot saying something that funny. The Mexican laughed too, before punching Scurvy hard on the arm again. I was still pissed that someone like this guy would have my life in his fumbling hands, but something told me I would need to get used to that. I walked the last hundred feet to the Number One Laundry on rubbery legs but at least I could laugh about it. I thought that an auspicious occasion like losing one's cherry would be a little more exciting but with each footfall, I felt only dread. Why was I doing this? I asked myself again, and still no answer came to mind.

Scurvy was first to the door. He opened it and entered, letting the spring snap it back on the point man. I followed them into the darkness of the hot, stuffy room. There wasn't much to it. There was a blonde coffee table in the middle of the room. It was ringed with beat-up old lawn chairs. Four rooms opened off the main room and were covered with plastic strips that hung ceiling to floor. They might have been blue and white before the dirt dulled them. The walls were plywood and were decorated with dozens of pictures of American movie stars that had been roughly cut from magazines and stuck to the wood with tape. When my eyes adjusted from the bright sunlight outside, I found myself staring into the steely gaze of Lee Marvin. Just the inspiration I needed, I thought. Lee Marvin would certainly know what to do in a whorehouse.

Scurvy plopped his ass into one of the lawn chairs, and I fought the urge to hose mine down before I, too, sat. We sat for a minute or so in awkward silence before the oft-mentioned Momma-san broke through the plastic strips of one of the doorways like she was leading her team through the crepe-paper hoop before a big game. The madam was a rotund little woman who was as wide as she was tall. She wore a blue housedress with bright yellow flowers, not unlike the housedresses I'd seen my own mother wear back home. Her shiny black hair was cinched up in a tight bun from which something akin to chopsticks protruded. She had brown sandals on her feet that actually looked stylish until I noticed they were made from plastic and not leather. She was bouncing from the Mexican to Scurvy. A hug here, a kiss on the cheek there, a strange look at me; she was everywhere. When she smiled at me, though, I noticed this swirling mass of yellow and gold swimming in a pool of mahogany filling her mouth. I almost puked when she kissed Scurvy wetly on the cheek.

"Hey Momma-san!" the amigo called. "You boo-coo happy see Number One GIs, huh? You bring us boo-coo cold beer boo-coo fast, OK?"

"GI got boo-coo money, Momma-san got boo-coo beer," she said before disappearing behind the plastic.

When she was gone, I leaned over to the Mexican.

"Those teeth," I said, making a face.

"Don't mean nothing, man," he answered. "It's called betel nut. They chew it like gum. It gives them a little buzz; sort of like six beers, you dig? It does fuck up a smile though, don't it?"

I asked my next New Guy question.

"What's all that boo-coo-ing?"

"It's French, FNG. Means 'a lot.'"

"Sort of like 'beaucoup' then, right?" I said, grinning to myself. What did I get myself drafted into—an army of idiots?

"I guess," the Mexican said. "Anyway, what it really means is we get some cold beer."

The old woman came waddling back into the parlor with three bottles of Budweiser looking like something out of a magazine ad. I might not have known much about getting laid, but I knew just about all there was to know about getting drunk. The beer looked frosty and inviting, as Madison Avenue would have said. Trailing behind Momma-san like three little ducklings were some very young looking girls. They tittered and giggled and acted generally like little girls, which, of course, they were. The uniform of the day seemed to be baggy, black silk pants that hung loosely around their legs and gauzy white blouses under which an occasional nipple swelled. Or was that the whole tit? I couldn't be sure. They quickly erased any notions I had of Suzy Wong or the Dragon Lady from Terry and the Pirates. I think we got Suzy Wrong instead. The odd gold tooth or two punctuated their incessant giggling and smiling. For kids, I thought that was pretty gross by itself. But what was really gross was these three little girls soon-to-be whores, living in squalor, with the sound of war all around them, and still they smiled. What the hell did they have to smile about? I was miserable here. Why weren't they? It made me think they knew something I didn't and it pissed me off.

I drank long and deep from the beer. It felt cold rolling down my throat and made me remember it had been almost a week since I'd had a drink. That was some kind of record. The other guys were laughing it up with the Vietnamese woman and her protégés while I finished my beer in three swallows. When the beer was gone I wanted the girls to vanish as well.

"Momma-san! More beer!" I said a little too loud. "Bring more beer for my friends and me."

The old woman looked at me kind of funny. At the time, I thought she was editorializing about how fast I drank the beer. Looking back, I figure she just hated my fucking guts. Before she stood, she looked at the Mexican. He nodded slightly and off she went.

"What the fuck was that?" I asked. "I'm paying for the party but you gotta give your approval for me to buy beer? Ain't this some shit?"

"Hey, New Guy, relax," the Mex said. "Enjoy

yourself. This ain't no race. You got 364 days left in the fucking 'Nam. Enjoy at least one of them."

The beers were brought out in a cheap foam cooler. Three chunks of ice chilled the bottles.

"OK," I said. "Now we can party." But Momma-san's foot was plunked right in the middle of the cooler. She looked at me with a frown and with her hand extended. I reached into my pocket and yanked out a ten-dollar bill. Her face changed immediately. *Now*, we could party.

After my third beer, the girls weren't looking any better.

"Hey guys, these girls drink beer or formula?" I asked. "Are we supposed to fuck them or burp them?"

"If you're like me, newbie, you'll do both."

"Hey, I used to have to cough up part of my lunch money a couple days a month to sponsor pagan babies. Maybe I already own one of these kids."

The Mexican got it because I probably sponsored his ass too. He looked at me and gave me a grudging laugh.

The air inside the shack was getting hotter and fouler as Scurvy and the point man lit cigarettes. I rubbed a cold bottle over my forehead and around my neck, trying to, at least, slow down the sweat but it was hopeless. Even as it took a little of the sting out of my new sunburn, it did nothing to calm the churning in my belly as the girls started their number. The scurvy guy already had his "date" playfully bouncing in his lap and the Mexican was playing with the ass of another. She playfully pushed his hand away but not before she let him get a good squeezing handful. My new girlfriend was standing near my right shoulder, occasionally mashing her crotch into my elbow. Either she was getting hot watching her friends play or she wanted this to be over as badly as I did. I looked up at her face. That was a big mistake. Her face was wide and round, like she'd been hit with a snow shovel. One of her upper teeth was gold and I could see one of her lowers was gone. Her nose was mashed against her face like a snout and her black hair hung off her, stringy and disheveled. I came to the simple conclusion that St. Louis didn't have enough Budweiser to make this girl look pretty. She gave me a crooked smile and started rubbing her tits against the back of my head. Even behind me, she was ugly. I yanked my head away and stood quickly. The girl ran quickly into one of the rooms.

The two other whores, both of whom could curdle milk with their faces, started a steady stream of jabber that must have been insults.

Scurvy looked like his dog had just been run over.

"Shit, New Guy, you're gonna fuck this up for all of us," he said, stroking the hair back from his date's pockmarked face.

Before I could respond, the point man grabbed my shirt and yanked me to my feet.

"Hey faggot, so these girls ain't no beauty queens. This ain't Hollywood either. You don't wanna fuck, don't fuck. But don't get your queer ass in our way."

Faggot? Queer ass? Who the fuck was this greaser talking to? I pulled away from him and got in his face.

"Don't forget who's paying for this party, beaner. You fucking assholes walk me through a minefield, use my money, drink my beer, and jerk me around three ways to Sunday but when I want a laugh, I'm a faggot? Fuck you, Mexican! Get that little bitch back out here and I'll show you who's a faggot."

Mamma-san had moved to the plastic and was watching the proceedings. When the point man gave her a nod she ducked behind the curtain and emerged with the now-sullen little girl.

"So you want to fuck, baby?" I snarled. "Where? Here? With your friends keeping score or do you have someplace private we can go to make plans for the prom?"

The Mexican mumbled some gibberish to her and she snatched my hand and led me into another airless room. Once through the curtain, she stripped off her shirt without ceremony and slipped out of the black pants. She lowered herself onto a low wooden bed covered with a thin mattress.

The room stunk of sweat and urine. She laid back, propped her head on a pillow and spread her legs. She looked even worse naked than she had with clothes on. I started to strip, got as far as my shirt and wanted only to get this over with. I dropped my pants and knelt in position. I waited for my dick to get hard but it didn't. I started to play with myself until it was stiff enough to make entry. The girl watched with utter disinterest, making me hate her even more. I started pumping, waiting for it to feel good; waiting for the indescribable sensation I had heard was part of this. It wasn't coming. I felt nothing but contempt building in me. I pumped hard and faster, sweating large drops that fell on the girl's face and chest. She remained oblivious, like she was dead. I needed her to move, to at least pretend. She was as still as the air. I fucked her even harder and was driving faster. The sweat poured into my eyes, tearing them.

"Fuck me you little bitch!" I demanded. "Fuck me!"

But she lay still as a stone. I felt my own climax building. I was going to lose. This little whore was going to beat me. I was giving her everything and she gave me nothing.

"Feel it?" I screamed in a convulsing spasm. "Feel me?"

I tried to kiss her, trying to make it more real, trying to imitate affection in a feeble try to get her to emote. But when I got near enough, she bit deeply into my lip. I jerked my mouth back, tasting blood. Her face was now hard and hate-filled. It was scowled in a twisted mask of hate.

She slid from under me and went to a corner of the room and splashed water on herself, washing me away.

Whatever made me think she was young? I wondered. My own eyes blinked away the sweat and the tears and filled with hatred of my own. I stood up, pulling my pants up quickly to cover myself. I reached into a pocket and pulled out some crumpled bills. I let them fall to the bed. She gathered them up and headed for the plastic.

She stopped and gave me one last glare.

"GI make no good fuckee," she said. "You boo-coo bad fuckee. GI make no good fuckee." Then she disappeared through the strips.

Like I needed her to tell me, I thought as I headed to the water pan. I wanted the water to wash more than my dick. I wanted it to bring back the guy I was. I wanted myself back, the self that I was slowly giving over to my fear.

A piece of mirror hung on the wall. I moved the cloth and looked at the face that stared back. My lip was swollen and split. My eye was already black and blue. This didn't look much like I'd been laid. Worse, I didn't recognize who the guy in the mirror was. I closed my eyes and tried to pray my way back to the old neighborhood, back to my old self, back to anywhere as long as I didn't have to walk through those plastic strips to face the other two Americans on the other side. The beer, the pain, the anger, the despair and the fear combined to make me dizzy. I tried to clear my head and shake away the notion that I'd spent a lot more than money in this vile little shack but I couldn't. I parted the plastic and heard a voice.

"Here he comes, Amigo," Scurvy said, his smile brimming with all the pride and the confidence of his invulnerable stupidity. "Welcome to the 'Nam, FNG."

If I thought losing my cherry was going to be the worst of my unholy baptism, I was wrong.

Three days later, I was at the head of a platoon of the guys called "grunts," patrolling south of the base. Three days in Vietnam, in the same unit as the legendary Mexican, the point man to beat all point men, and I'm walking out a hundred yards ahead of everybody else. Reports of my performance in the Number One Laundry had made their way through the platoon and I learned the practical lesson that not being liked makes it easier to be chosen to walk point. The point man, it seems, was only "the" point when it counted.

Sort of like being a starting pitcher in the majors, I

reasoned.

One of the few things that had sunk in during my pre-Vietnam indoctrination was that the life expectancy of a point man in combat was somewhat less than that of the average victim of a hit and run by a tractor trailer. While my college English classes taught me how to name "hyperbole," my street smarts had taught me how to recognize bullshit for what it was.

But still, I thought, no sense in bucking the odds on the first day out. So I had started my walk like a wary panther, choosing literally every step with studied care. I was checking for vipers and snipers and snares and mantraps. Little did it matter to me that I was still within sight of the main gate of the base. I grew tired of that pretty quick when the platoon threatened to shoot me in the ass if I didn't hurry up so I stepped up the pace. Two hours later, I was boiling in a heat vastly different from anything else I'd ever experienced. The sweat was sheeting out from under my steel helmet and I thought I could hear the rushing sound of my brains boiling. The sweat had found its way into my eyes and the sun was beating on my soul, as each footfall became another exercise in torture. I was so wilted I was no longer scared. I no longer even gave a shit where I was walking. Only fate brought me back to consciousness.

Just ahead I saw some beautiful shade. To get to it,

all I had to do was scale a sheer twenty-foot wall of baked dirt the other guys told me was laterite. I stood at the bottom of the wall, wanting to cry. The shade was at the top of this cliff, but I was too fucking tired to scale it.. I searched both flanks of the wall for an alternate route but impassable brush kept bringing me back to the wall.

Fuck it, I thought. I'll get over this bad boy. I slung my rifle over my shoulder and looked for the first foothold. As I started to climb, I glanced back and saw the rest of the platoon watching me. I couldn't hear the whispered conversations but I saw the hulking platoon sergeant, talking to the Mexican.

"He'll never make it," the Mexican sneered.

"A case of beer says he does," the sarge countered.

I was up about ten feet and the going was getting tougher, especially with my sweat turning the dry dirt to mud beneath my grip. I slid out my bayonet and stabbed it into the rock-like dirt to pull myself to a tight little crevice just wide enough for me to stick a toe in. From there, it got easy. I wanted to scream out "fuck a bunch of cliffs" but quietly continued my climb. My hands gripped the top edge of the wall and I started to pull myself up. Below and behind, the sarge whispered to the point man.

"I think this kid's gonna be all right."

The Mexican wasn't convinced.

"So he can't fuck," the sarge smiled. "He sure can climb."

While the two soldiers debated my worth, I was making a discovery of my own.

I smelled something weird first. Then I heard the voices. As I crawled over the edge and into the brush that covered the plateau, I saw them. Two little Vietnamese guys were sitting around a small fire that had some kind of thatch over it. One was dressed in black shorts and shower sandals. The other guy was dressed in a black silky shirt and had a kerchief around his neck. He wore some kind of weird sneaker-looking boots. Between them sat a long black machine gun resting on its bipod legs. A circular drum style magazine sat atop it. It didn't look like any kind of machine gun I'd ever seen, but I didn't exactly have a lot of experience in that regard. I thought these guys had to be ours. I hadn't exactly been quiet scaling the wall so they must have known I was here. But if they did, neither showed it. I thought I better check. So just as the other guys were massing at the base of the wall, I climbed back over the edge. The point man was closest to me.

"Hey Mexican," I whispered, "we got any friendlies around?"

"Fuck no. Ain't nobody else dumb enough to be out on a hot motherfucker like this."

"Well then who are the two guys up here with the fire? They got a new machine gun with a drum clip on the top."

"Oh fuck, New Guy!" The urgency in the Mexican's voice made me feel like hot ginger ale had replaced my blood.

"That's fucking Charlie with a Russian machine gun. Kill those gooks, new guy. Waste 'em before they turn the gun on you."

I slid back over the rim of the cliff and sighted down my M-16.

How the fuck could I be in this position? I asked myself.

How the fuck could an FNG sneak up on the meanest jungle fighters in the fucking world?

I closed my eyes for a second giving God one last chance to alert the VC they were going to die.

Please God; don't make me do this, I begged.

I opened my eyes to God's answer. They were still there, still oblivious to my presence; still about to die. I sucked in one last breath to steady my aim. Only then did I see the faces of my victims-to-be. One of them was facing me. His face was brown and deeply lined. He was jabbering about something and then his face broke into a broad smile. His mouth was full of that same fucked up morass of betel nut and gold teeth I saw at the whorehouse.

"Fuck you," I whispered.

The crack of the bullet pulverized the tattered walls of my moral universe at the same time it exploded into the jaw of the VC. His face erupted in a red mess of blood and bone. When I saw the backside of his jawbone break out of his mouth, my breakfast spewed out onto my hands and my rifle. I rose to kneeling as the other VC jumped to his feet. I squeezed again and the Duffy I was died as certainly as my enemy did. One bullet thwacked low on his shoulder blade and the other went high and into his neck. I was paralyzed with my rifle still against my shoulder. The VC turned toward me, gripping his throat as though his stubby little fingers could stanch the flow of the torrent of blood pouring out the big exit wound in his throat. His eyes looked right through me; maybe into some calmer place he might be headed. But I saw his eyes. I saw into the final seconds of that man's life as it gushed out the bullet hole I'd put in him.

Would there ever be absolution for this, I wondered, even though I knew the answer.

The Mexican's bullet to the heart put the VC down in the dirt where thousands of flies were already circling his dead comrade. I puked as the blood flowed and pooled in the dry dust and darkened it to mud. My head was spinning as fast as my stomach was churning.

What was happening? Who was I? Where had the

real me gone? So much was happening so fast. I came to this place a little tainted but a good, decent guy. Now I was fouled with my own puke, not even bothering to shoo away the flies whipping around me. Less than twenty feet away lay two bodies that used to be men killed by my hand, their blood pooling on the dry ground. I had no idea who I was right now but I knew the words "good" and "decent" no longer applied. Dante couldn't have painted any clearer picture of it for me. I was in hell.

And all this just for failing ROTC.

Fuck me.

CHAPTER TWO

WHEN KINDNESS IS WEAKNESS

The white ball of burning phosphorous hissed like a snake as it slid through the falling rain. The flare cast an eerie silver light that silhouetted the two guerrillas stumbling through the shallows at the river's edge. I deliberately stared into the flare to generate a little night blindness. Now I saw nothing but a white blur. I yanked back the trigger on the machine gun and the M-60 spit a hundred rounds that stitched across the river. I was hitting everything but the targets. The platoon noticed.

"Drop your sight, FNG!"

"They're on this bank asshole, not the other bank!"

"Who's shooting – Ray-fucking-Charles?"

The catcalls dissolved in the steady rain as I sent another burst into mid river, nowhere close to the targets.

I'd tasted the bitter bile of killing and I resolved that I wouldn't taste it again. So I blasted another hundred rounds behind the fleeing VC as they ducked into a pier of sampans and junks down stream. I eased off the stock of the 60 and took a deep breath. I inhaled the smell of chewing tobacco and knew the sarge was in the bunker.

"You blind, kid?" he asked.

"No, Sarge, I just looked into that flare and lost my night vision."

"Then you worse than blind, Duffy. You stupid."

Before I could say anything, the sarge was gone, leaving me alone in the bunker. I was letting my adrenalin level get back to normal when I heard a voice from the hole next to the bunker.

"Gee, Duff, I guess you missed them. Nice shooting."

Coming from any other voice in the platoon I knew that would have been an insult but coming from "Chicago," I recognized it as a compliment.

He was the closest thing I had to a friend in the platoon. He was new like me and he'd seen my reaction when I was forced to kill two Viet Cong two weeks ago. While the other guys treated me like a hero, he saw the revulsion that had filled me when I looked at my victims. So after the other guys had taken turns congratulating me, he approached me.

"Some sick shit, ain't it?" he said. "They make us kill and think that will make us like killing. It's even sicker that the rest of the sheep in the flock think it's a good thing."

"I close my eyes and I can see that face just before I pulled the trigger," I said. "One minute the guy is alive and the next he's dead because I shot him. I still can't believe I really did that."

We talked a long time about the butchery of it all, of the killing from ambush and the gloating when we did. We wondered what was happening to us in the blaze of all the bullets and sea of blood. And we wondered if the other guys were normal before they got to Vietnam, before they started acting like psychos.

It was just more than a month that I'd been in country and I saw a guy with dental pliers he said he used to yank the gold teeth from the dead. Another guy sharpened his knife continually to make it easier to take souvenirs from the bodies. I learned to kill from ambush, who to shoot to make sure none of the gooks got away, and how to set booby traps to kill anyone hapless enough to trip an unseen wire. It was one thing to shoot someone shooting at me but this science of killing just made the whole thing look like an army of nut jobs committing murder under the guise of patriotism. The more we talked the angrier we got.

"I may not be able to change the army," I told him,

"but it sure as hell isn't going to change me."

I refused to admit to myself the ways I'd already changed, the ways I'd already evolved as though ignoring the change would mean it didn't happen. They got me to kill once but it wouldn't happen again. So when we moved out of the jungle and on to bridge security, I prayed I wouldn't be confronted with the need to kill. Those prayers, like so many others, were answered with silence. But two human beings were alive because I chose not to kill them and that was a start. The other guys could call them "dinks" and "slopes" and "gooks" but they were still living, breathing people. I wouldn't surrender any more of my humanity to the madness.

When morning broke, so did the torrent of insults about my shooting.

"Your ass is going to be transferred to a dog unit," one said, "but not K-9. You shipping out to C 'n I."

"Hey asshole," another one said, "one of them wastes a GI and that kill is on your ass. This ain't no game, dickhead. The gooks are playing for keeps and you're out here fucking around."

But I didn't give a shit what they said. I'd decided. No more killing.

The bridge duty was called a "cake job," an easy one after pounding through the jungle. We sat around all day,

cleaning our rifles and guns and babysitting the bridge at
night. Anywhere you saw Chicago, you saw a gaggle of
Vietnamese kids. He gave them stuff from the c-ration
boxes we had and tried to teach them some English. Our
sergeant didn't like it and told him so.

"Hell, Sarge, they're just kids; hungry kids looking
for a handout. They ain't hurting anybody."

"A baby rattlesnake grows up to be a big rattlesnake,
new guy," the sarge reminded him. "Don't forget that."

I got into the act a little myself. One of the kids came
around every day to shine my boots and I gave him food in
payment. But not everyone felt the same.

"This ain't no fucking orphanage, Duffy, so you keep
those little fuckers away from my bunker."

On our third day at the bridge the sarge came by in the
heat of the day.

"I'm thinking you boys need a little work on the 60,"
he said. I knew from the look on his face he didn't think my
terrible shooting was an accident. So instead of lolling in
the shade somewhere like the rest of the platoon, Chicago
and I were in the hot sun stripping the machine gun down,
cleaning it, firing it, and cleaning it again. I fired a few
thousand rounds at shit floating down the river. When the
sarge was satisfied, I broke down the gun again and made
it shine before repeating the exercise on the next batch of

floating debris. The gun grease and the cleaning oil were burning on my hands and the sun was doing the same to my neck but we repeated the exercise over and over. A crowd gathered to watch the show. They laughed and jeered when I shot well over a tree limb floating in the river.

"Maybe we need to start all over again," the sarge said. I got the message. I took a breath and squeezed on the trigger, ripping the wood to splinters.

"Well maybe you got the hang of this, Duffy," the sarge said. "I'll make a troop out of your green ass yet."

No you won't, Sarge, I thought. No you won't.

Our cake duty ended midway through the fourth day. The sarge came to my bunker with some disturbing news.

"Back to the bush, soldier. Get your shit together and go up to the point with Mex. He's rotating back to the World soon and he needs a replacement. You the man, son."

"Me? Are you kidding, Sarge? Tonto couldn't replace Mex. The guy's a fucking legend. How the hell do I follow that act?"

"You a smart-assed college boy, Duffy. You'll find a way."

He walked off with a smile that said 'don't fuck with me ever again, boy.'

In the next foxhole, Chicago packed his rucksack as one of his little Vietnamese friends stood looking with a sad face.

"The sarge is trying to get me killed," I said. "He's making me a point man.

"Just go with the flow," he said. "The Mex is still up there with you. You'll be all right."

"Yeah? Your ass is back in the pack and mine is hanging out to dry on point. It's pretty goddamn easy for you to say."

"Hey, I didn't put you up there. The lifer sarge did. He's the bad guy, not me."

I threw the rest of my shit in the pack and moved up to the front of the column. The Mex was waiting for me.

"Hey guys," he said, "lookie here. It's that Jose Feliciano motherfucker from the machine gun bunker. Man, you better keep those eyes open up here with me and I ain't even bullshittin' you."

"Don't worry about me. I'll take care of myself."

"Worry about you? Fuck that shit, Duffy. I don't care a lick about your sorry ass. Just don't do anything that fucks up my day."

The chorus of charging handles being pulled and bolts sliding rounds in place signaled the move was on. I was still sulking about being on point when the point man grabbed my shoulder. He didn't become a walking legend by not being observant.

"Look, motherfucker, I don't care dog shit about what happens to your sorry ass, but when you're backing me up you better soldier. You got that? Now put a round in that chamber before I put a round in your ass."

I shook free of his grasp and gave him my meanest look. He just chambered his weapon and stared back and I knew he wasn't fooling around. I pulled back the handle of the M-16 but when it slid forward to put the bullet in the chamber a loud explosion replaced the quiet click I'd expected. I looked at the rifle confused by what was going on and then I saw the point squad scrambling into the drainage ditches on both sides of the road. What had I done?

"Hey asshole, get off the fucking road unless you want your nuts blown off," the Mex yelled. I heard him and I understood what he said but I didn't move.

"What's going on?" I asked.

"How the fuck do I know? I was standing next to you, dickhead."

I crawled into the ditch thankful I hadn't screwed up. We waited for what seemed like an hour. The wait ended when the sarge strolled up.

"Duffy! On your feet!"

I stepped out of the ditch. Ready to disclaim responsibility for anything, not knowing what I might be charged with.

"Come with me, Duffy. You got a job to do."

"I thought my job was on point with the Mex."

"Now you got a new job, soldier. Your boy bought it back here. One of his little gook friends gave him a box that had a booby-trapped grenade inside. Blew the shit out of him."

The sarge's lips were still moving but I stopped hearing after "blew the shit out of him." How? When? Where? All the questions cascaded over my mind as I tried to take in the meaning of the sarge's words. Ahead of him, near his bunker, streaks of gray smoke hung in the air. The platoon had recovered from their collective reaction to the explosion and stood on the road looking at me like I was covered with cow shit.

"What happened, Sarge? Where's Chicago? What's going on?"

"You couldn't see the other night and now you can't fucking hear! Wake the fuck up, Duffy! Your friend is dead. He's gone."

We walked up on some turned over dirt and there he was, still smoking from the blast that ripped out most of his chest. His face was charred and unrecognizable.

"Oh my God, Sarge. Are you sure that's him?"

"Yeah Duffy. We're sure. Now take this and bag him

up." The sergeant held a green rubber bag out to me.

"Do what?" I asked with tears seeping from the corners of my eyes. I started to turn away but the sarge had a firm grip on my shoulder.

"He's your friend, Duffy, and he's dead. You need to put the body in this bag so we can load him on a chopper."

"I can't do it …"

"The fuck you can't! You will do it, Duffy, and you'll do it now."

The tone of his voice told me we weren't negotiating so I walked over to the smoking corpse and knelt down. The smell of burnt flesh filled my nostrils and I retched into the road. I couldn't bring myself to touch it, like death might be contagious. But I had no choice. The sarge stood over me as the rest of the guys looked on. The flies were on the corpse in force and they buzzed around my face spending way too much time near my mouth. I thought I might puke again but I caught it and swallowed. I wasn't going to give these psychos anything else to laugh about. I started out trying to fit the body into the bag but pieces kept coming off in my hands. I was up to my wrists in blood when one of the other guys knelt with me.

"Lift him up," he said and I did as he asked. Then he slid the bag over the remnant of Chicago's head. "Now the feet." I lifted and the bag slid over the blown up body.

"I got way too fucking much practice at this," he said. "It's always easier to put the bag over the body instead of the body into the bag."

He stood and walked off, leaving me on my knees in the mud made by my dead friend's blood. I wanted to pray but I had no idea what to ask for. My world had changed too fast for me to keep up. I had no idea what was going on.

"Zip up the bag." The sarge's voice reminded me where I was. I pulled the zipper up and stood.

"Walk with me," he said.

We walked away from the body bag. The men had all turned their heads away from death and busied themselves with details for the move. The sergeant spoke in a steady, reasoned voice. This time, I heard every word.

"You in hell now, boy. Make no mistake about it The old rules don't count no more. You can't run no game in this place. The game runs you. You play only to win. You can't never lose – never. You understand me boy?

"You and your man thought you could be nice guys and feed these little killers. But this ain't the world, my man. This is hell. This is the motherfucking 'Nam. You might be as badass on your block, but you ain't seen nothing like this shit. The men kill you. The women kill you. The kids kill you. The land will kill you. You got nothing but your own self and these other guys to keep you alive. And that's all that matters- staying alive. Kindness don't cut it here, Duffy. Kindness is weakness and weakness kills your ass. Don't never forget that, you hear?"

I heard and now I heeded. I made myself a promise as I walked up to take my place behind the Mex. No one will ever kneel in the blood and the mud and the puke to put me in a bag – no one, not ever. I was going to win this fucking game, even if I hardly knew the rules.

Before he walked off, the sergeant gave me one more bit of news.

"I saw your lips moving when you were bagging your buddy, Duffy. So I suppose you were praying. Don't bother. No God, no Buddha, no Allah … none of them be hanging around this shit hole. Don't be wasting God's time with your bullshit. Just keep your weapon clean. Cover your ass and cover the ass of the guy on your left and right. That's all the praying you need."

Amen to that, Sarge, I thought. A-fucking-men to that.

CHAPTER THREE

A COWARD FOR A MINUTE

It didn't take too long for me to suffer my first wound. It wasn't to an arm or leg or head or torso. It was worse. It was my pride.

It began when the sergeant gave me a new assignment.

"Duffy, grab your shit and head on over to the other Scout hooch."

"Scouts? Those crazy bastards with the mohawks and the weird weapons? What am I supposed to do over there?"

"They had a couple guys hit and a guy on R&R. They're short some grunts so they need a guy for one mission and I thought you'd be the prefect dude to fill in."

"Me? Why me? There's a lot better soldiers in the platoon than me. Those guys are crazy. I ain't a Scouts soldier."

"You're right, Duffy. You ain't no Scouts troop. Those guys are real soldiers, son. They're the best and if you keep your mouth shut and your eyes open, you might learn something."

"You're just trying to get me killed, Sarge."

He stopped fiddling with his gear and looked at me.

"No, Duffy. I'm not trying to get you killed. I'm trying to keep you alive. Go out with Scouts. Watch how they soldier. See how they operate. Learn how to survive. Besides, Scouts don't like to engage the enemy. They observe and report. So it seems like a perfect place to put you, seeing as how you got this thing about killing gooks."

This was utter bullshit, I thought. These Scout guys were gung-ho lifers always looking for a fight. The sarge is screwing with me because he thinks I'm yellow. But there was no arguing with him. I grabbed my gear and started off with the stony, silent stares of the other guys watching me leave. To argue now would just prove to the squad that I'm a coward. I didn't know which scared me more: going on the mission or staying back and being branded yellow.

"Hey Duffy," the sergeant called. "Make us proud."

Sure thing, Sarge, as long as the mission doesn't make me dead, I thought.

I got to the Scout hooch and saw five guys dressed in camouflaged fatigues working on weapons I'd never seen before. One of the guys looked up from his work.

"You the leg the sarge sent us?"

Leg? I wondered. What the hell is a "leg"?

"Yeah, I'm the leg."

"All righty then. I'm running the mission. We're going to be out three nights. We take off at dusk, fake a few landings and jump off just about the time it's too dark for Mr. Charles to see us."

My face must have given away that I had no idea who Mr. Charles was.

"Charlie ... the VC ... the fuckin' enemy, FNG. Didn't they teach you anything over in that leg company?"

"I just never heard of the VC referred to as 'mister' before," I said.

"When you've seen them operate up close like we have, grunt, you get a certain respect for their skills. Thus, we call them mister around here."

Wow, I thought, respect wasn't a word I heard much in this shithole.

"What do we do when we get where we're going?" I asked.

"We wait and we watch. There's a trail we're going to eyeball. We think the bad guys are moving supplies down it."

"What if you're right? They probably have more guys than we do."

"They always have more guys than we do, troop. That's why we just watch. We get a bead on them and call it in. The gunships or the artillery do the rest. We're just spectators."

"But what if …"

"There ain't no what ifs. We wait and we watch. Don't fuck-up the mojo with no bad vibes."

Waiting and watching didn't sound half-bad but I still had a lot of what ifs running through my mind no matter what that did to the mojo.

"Let me make this simple for you," the leader said. "Just do what we do and you'll be fine."

The other guys thought that was funny.

"Yeah," one of them said, "that's why we're a man down – cuz everything is just fine."

A guy sitting next to the radio picked up the handset.

"Bird's on the way," he said. "Zero five minutes out."

The leader looked at me.

"Jump up and down," he said.

"What?"

"Jump up and down. It's pretty simple."

I started to say something but the leader grabbed me.

"I'm going to say this once. We got five guys. That's all. You're one of those five. You do what you are told when you are told. You don't ask questions. You don't give me no back talk. When I say jump up and down, jump the fuck up and down."

I did as I was told.

"See?" he said. "You're too noisy. You got too much shit in that ruck."

He started pulling stuff out of my rucksack.

"This stuff works when you got a whole platoon with you, troop. It don't work on a recon mission. We travel fast and we travel light but most of all, we travel quietly. You got chow for three days?"

I nodded.

"Make sure you got water. You don't need all that ammo but you damned sure need water."

He handed me two more canteens.

"Keep six magazines of ammo in a bandoleer. They won't make noise that way. "

I did as I was told. The other three guys finished working on their weapons and rose to shoulder their packs. Show time, I thought. Let's see what you've got, Duffy.

The helicopter barely touched the ground before it was airborne again. The chopper rides were as close as I could get to solitude. The noise of the rotors made talking impossible and the air got cooler as the bird climbed higher, offering some temporary relief from the stifling heat on the ground. Three thousand feet over the jungle, I could almost forget about the chaos lurking below. The dwindling light cast long shadows from the clusters of jungle that looked like green brocade from this height. My grandmother had a couch tufted like the landscape below. The leader leaned in to my ear.

"Don't drift too far away. Keep your head in the game, troop." And just like that I was back in the war.

It was near dark when the helicopter dipped and shot down to a clearing. Then it rose rapidly and repeated the dive a minute or so later. Two more dives and the pilot turned to us and gave a thumbs-up sign. The leader leaned in again.

"That's our cue," he yelled. "Next landing is for real."

I nodded and got ready. The chopper flattened the grass below us and the guys started jumping out. I made my leap and the leader followed. Seconds later the darkness and the quiet washed over us. We knelt in the tall grass until the leader rose and started toward the tree line. I started to follow but one of the guys grabbed me by the rucksack and signaled to me to wait. The leader disappeared into the jungle. A minute later he reappeared and signaled for us to follow. The cool air I felt during the ride was a faded memory now. The jungle trapped the heat and wrapped around me like a wet wool blanket. I mimicked the guy in front of me, walking carefully among the rotting leaves and tangled vines, all the while trying and failing to keep the sweat from my eyes. I was desperate to show these scout guys I could soldier even as I wondered why it mattered. We moved deeper into the jungle for the longest half hour of my life. No one spoke. No one checked a map. No one did anything but walk. I gave up trying to keep my eyes free of sweat and just followed blindly behind the man in front of me. The darkness this deep in the jungle was almost tangible. I could see nothing. I could only feel. The only life I could sense were the flying pests buzzing around me but if there was one thing the army did well, it was repel things and the bug repellent kept the miniature buzzards from landing. I tried to keep sight of the guy in front of me but I followed the slight sound of his movement more than any sight of him. I almost tripped over him before I realized he'd stopped. He snapped his head around but eased a bit when he saw it was me. He motioned for me to kneel and we both did. Soon, the leader appeared and motioned to the other guy to head to the left. He motioned me to the right. I started off, still trying to find the quietest way through the riot of jungle that was wrapped around my ankles. I went about five meters when I saw the outline of one of the other scouts. He motioned me five meters to his right and I found a place to flop. A few minutes later the leader appeared next to me as if teleported. He made no sound and I had no sight. He leaned into my ear and whispered.

"The trail is about twenty meters to your front. Lay here. Stay awake and remember everything you see. Hopefully, it won't be much." Then he was gone as swiftly and silently as he'd appeared. I looked to my right, trying to see if there was anyone there but couldn't make anything out in the blackness. Would they leave me out here on the flank alone? I wondered, but gave up wondering when I knew it didn't really matter. There were only five of us so where you were was pretty much immaterial. I tried to make myself small and comfortable at the same time but soon realized the two were mutually exclusive. I drank a little water and reapplied the bug repellent and just that fast, was out of things to do. So I did as I was told. I lay there.

At some point in the night, some thin slivers of gray light started to slide through the trees and puddle on the jungle floor. I still couldn't see any trail or anything else but tree trunks and bushes but if the leader said it was out there it must be. Time for another sip of water, I thought, and started to open the canteen when I heard the rustle of brush. I looked out to where the trail was supposed to be but saw nothing. I started to open the canteen again when something hit my cheek. I looked to my left and one of the scouts had moved a little closer. I could faintly see him pointing out to the front. I was going to tell him I heard the same noise he did but then I knew I needn't bother.

I saw the guy come straight toward me. He was small and I thought he would walk right over me. Then he turned and walked from my left to my right. He was wary but not stealthy. I knew I could shoot him from this distance and knew just as well that I wouldn't. The man disappeared but I heard the noise coming from in front of me. Here was another small man, walking through the shafts of light along the same path the other man had taken. Behind him, came another and then another and then a steady stream of guys. They all had rifles. Some of them carried them at the ready. Others had them slung over their shoulders. Some carried them like a hobo stick, holding the barrel and resting the stock on their shoulders. Then some came carrying poles, a man at each end. Something like a hammock was slung from the pole. Then came a guy with an American M-60 machine gun. Fucking gook, I thought, he took that from a dead GI. And they kept coming, for a long time. Thirty, forty, fifty guys and still they came. I had never seen this many of the enemy. And they were close; close enough for me to hear them whisper to each other. They were moving swiftly but quietly; utterly unaware that anyone was watching them. But what if they became aware? What if I gave us away? What if they heard me? My heart was not just beating fast. It pounded. I'd never heard it beat so loudly. Would they hear me? What if one of them comes over here to take a piss? We'd be dead in minutes. There would be no saving us. We would probably never be found. Worse yet, what if they captured me? What fate would await a prisoner? Would I ever be heard from again? The buzzing of the mosquitoes hurt my ears. Could the gooks hear the buzzing? Would the buzzing give me away? My heart beat faster. I could feel the surge of blood shooting out of it. Before I knew it I was trembling, shaking with fear and still the fucking enemy kept coming. How the fuck many had already passed? I stopped counting at something in the 50s but how long ago was that? Is this the entire fucking VC army or what? I tried to find my rifle but knew I couldn't stop shaking long enough to use it. My Jesus, I was going to die, right here, right now, in this terrible fucking tract of jungle no one would ever find on a map. Just when I thought I would shake so loud as to be heard, I felt the weight on top of me. Who the fuck is that? I wondered. The camouflaged arm I saw meant it was a scout. He was laying on me to still the tremors. But his weight was suffocating. What was happening to me?

I didn't see any more movement on the trail and the scout rolled off me. The stillness swept back over the jungle and signaled the peril had passed. He was close enough for me to see him smiling.

"Dude," he whispered. "You stink."

Stink? I thought. What the fuck is he talking about. Then I smelled it too. What the hell was that? I rolled over to take a look around and felt something between my legs. I moved again and it hit me. I shit my pants. I was so scared I shit my pants. The shame heated my face. Quivering in the face of fear was one thing. Being scared shitless was another. I am a coward, I realized. There's no denying it now. How does anyone recover from this kind of shame? I wanted to dig a hole and bury myself in it. The noise of the explosions shook me from my self-loathing. Like a ghost, the leader reappeared by my side.

"Hear that?" he whispered. "That's big-assed artillery shells raining all over that gook ass. We did the job, man. We found them and someone else is fucking them up." The whiteness of his teeth showed his wide smile even in the darkness.

"You did the job," I hissed. "I just laid here and shook and shit my pants like a little girl. I didn't do anything cuz I was too goddamned scared."

"We were all scared, man. You ain't alive if that shit

don't scare you. There were nearly a hundred guys walking within twenty meters of us. That's enough to scare the shit out of anybody." He grinned and I knew he wasn't making a joke.

"Let's get the fuck out of here before they come back and find out who blew their ass in."

We got to our feet and moved in the opposite direction of the explosions. He moved faster than before and made a little more noise but I figured it was worth it to put some distance between the bad guys and us. Each step was one closer to safety but each step for me started some grating between my legs. I'd shaken some of the shit out of my pants but the residue remained. I put it out of my mind though and kept up with the GIs as we moved away from the artillery barrage.

It wasn't too bad at first. I tried keeping my legs as far apart as I could to cut down the friction but it was hopeless. After a few hours, I felt like I had sand paper between my legs. But I didn't slow down. The team was moving fast and I was still part of the team. I wondered if anyone had ever called time out in a war to change shitty pants. I kept the vision of a zebra-striped ref in my head to keep my mind off the growing pain. It didn't work. Soon, the sand paper feeling gave way to one of ground glass, slicing and dicing the inside of my thighs. The sun made the walk hot enough, but it wasn't long before I started to feel like I was cooking from the inside out. I wanted to save as much water as I could, not knowing where we were going or when I'd get refilled but even when I drank, my mouth felt like it was stuffed with a tennis ball. Instead of just getting hot, I started feeling dizzy as we made our way through the jungle. Don't stop, I told myself, soldier through this. Shitting your pants can't be fatal. But it almost was.

By the time we found the stream, I was really hurting. The leader sent the guys to provide security above and below our position before I took my boots off and then he helped me out of my shitty pants .

"Damn, son, you're burning up. Take it easy for a few minutes. We gotta get your ass outta here ASAP."

I couldn't respond. I just sat in the water and let its coolness surround me and take some of the sting out of the heat that was searing me. I laid my head back and closed my eyes.

The next thing I knew the leader was dragging me up on to the stream bank.

"Jesus, Duffy, you can't fucking sleep in a creek. What the hell's the matter with you?"

I was too busy spitting and coughing up water to answer. In no time, the heat returned to my body. The leader left me on the bank and hurried over to the radioman. I couldn't hear what he said and didn't really care. I was beyond caring about anything except the fire that was all over me. I closed my eyes. I didn't open them until the dirt and dust from the medevac chopper roiled around me. The team helped me on to the bird and scrambled in behind me. I closed my eyes again.

When I woke up, I was in a room so bright the light hurt my eyes. I had needle in each arm and my legs were propped up in stirrups. A nurse was putting ice bags all around my torso.

"Hello there soldier," she said. I wanted to respond but I couldn't move my lips. I couldn't move anything, in fact. So I tried to smile.

"You'll be feeling better when the antibiotics kick in," she said. "Until then, just get some rest while we try to get that fever down."

I tried to speak again but the nurse put some ice chips in my mouth. It felt heavenly.

I opened my eyes and saw the hulking figure of the sarge standing over me.

"Welcome back to the living, Duffy."

"Good to be back, I guess," I said, my mouth and lips working this time. "How long was I asleep?"

"Almost two days."

"What? Two days? What happened?"

"You rubbed your legs raw walking around with that shit in your pants. Vietnam is like a big Petri dish. Bacteria grow like a mother. You opened a wound and it got infected. Took a while to fight it off. But don't get lazy. Your ass is mine again day after tomorrow."

"I can't wait."

"And I got a message for you from the Scout guys. They said you can go out with them any time, anywhere."

"But, Sarge, did they tell you what happened? Did they …"

"Fuck yeah, Duffy, they told me. But there ain't one of us in this whole god-forsaken shit hole that ain't been a coward for a minute or two. But their leader said you soldiered and didn't whine or gripe. You're getting there, Duffy. You're going to be a soldier whether you like it or not."

Like it or not, I thought, like it or not …

CHAPTER FOUR

IF

If ... two shitty little letters forming one shitty little word.

How could such brevity carry so much meaning, so many variables, so many possibilities, so little certainty?

If it hadn't been raining that morning ... if Charlie Company hadn't walked into that ambush ... if we didn't have to rappel into that patch of jungle ... if my piece-of-shit M-16 hadn't jammed ...

If ... if ... if... so many goddamned "ifs" had to bleed together to put us in the scary fucking place we're in now.

All we knew was that Charlie Company was getting hammered and they were in deep shit. They needed help and they needed it fast. They were getting blasted in some thick jungle too dense to bring in choppers. So the call came in to bring rappelling gear, as we'd be sliding in to the rescue. We were hustled into birds and were on site in about fifteen minutes. The din of the battle was already pounding in my ears as we approached so I knew this was going to be some heavy-duty contact.

As soon as the choppers started to hover, they started taking fire. Green and white tracers sliced crazy patterns in the sky but I didn't waste any time watching the show. The sarge went first, then me, and then–well, then somebody. Who the fuck knows who? I grabbed the rope just as a tracer shot passed our bird. Hanging on a swinging rope was not the place to be when being shot at so I decided I'd take the express to the ground and brake myself just before touching down. But the rope felt like it was greased with oil and my effort to brake didn't work. I slammed into the dirt way faster than the training manuals said was "acceptable." I hit so goddamned hard my teeth hurt and my head jammed up into my helmet. But that was nothing compared to the electric bolt of hurt that shot up my leg from my ankle. Ahead of me, the sarge was charging balls to the wall toward the sound of the shooting. I tried to follow but fell flat on my face, my ankle telling me to go fuck myself. As the sarge disappeared, I grabbed the laces on my boot and pulled them as tight as I could. There wouldn't be any timeout or substitution in this shit. You just soldier on. I started off on a heavy limp in the direction the sarge took. The sound of the bullets zinging overhead told me I was getting close to the action. But crouching low and limping are not two activities that are complementary. I broke through some bamboo and the clutching, grabbing tangle we called wait-a-minute vines into a thinner patch of jungle. I heard the frenzied screams of soldiers at war--one guy screaming for ammo, another directing machine gun fire, another begging for a medic. I caught sight of the sarge on one knee next to a palm tree, sweeping his rifle back and forth, picking off bad guys as they tried to sneak forward. One pop from his rifle and a target would fall; another pop and another went down. It was like he was born to kill people.

The pain in my ankle was radiating up my leg now and every instinct was telling me to just recoil in the fetal position and wait for this shit to be over. But something else told me I couldn't. So I did what the sarge was doing. I knelt and killed "targets," which is a sterilized way of saying I killed human beings. I dropped two and saw a third come out from underneath some brush. He was lining up a shot at the sarge but I got him in my sights and fired at him. At least I thought I fired at him. Instead of that comfortable feeling of the rifle recoiling, I simply heard a "click." I pulled the trigger again and got the same empty sound. We're in the middle of the worst fighting I'd ever been in and now I have what feels like a broken ankle and no weapon. The gook dropped the sarge with one shot, knocking him over backward. I grabbed at my belt and snatched a grenade from the harness. I threw it at the gook as hard as I could, never once thinking to pull the pin. The steel ball hit the gook in the chest and sent him flying back. I scrambled over to the sarge's body and grabbed his rifle. The gook realized the grenade wasn't going to blow his ass to Buddha and he got aggressive again. But his reprieve was brief because now I was armed and sent two rounds into the center mass of his chest. Threat removed, I moved to the sarge and saw him bleeding from his arm and chest.

"Fuck, Sarge, you caught two," I said as I was grabbing at my first aid pack.

"Never use your own bandage, Duffy," he growled. "They should have taught you that shit stateside."

"Two bullet holes and you still can't stop lecturing." I took his pack and opened it.

"One bullet, two holes," he said. "The round went through my arm and into my chest."

This was beyond my limited ability to deal with. "Medic!"

"Fuck the medic, Duffy! He's gonna be busy with serious shit. Wrap the bandage around my arm and make sure it covers both holes. And tie it as tight as you can to help slow the bleeding. And don't be a pussy about tying it tight either."

Trying to please the un-pleasable almost took my mind off the chaos still swirling around us. I pulled the straps on the bandage particularly hard to inflict a little pain on the guy who got me into this shit, and I saw a glint of gold stuck in a hole in the sarge's chest. The bullet didn't penetrate very far into his chest.

"That bullet didn't go very far into your chest, Sarge. Does it hurt?"

"It's a goddamned bullet from an AK 47, asshole. How do you think it feels?"

I thought I saw a hint of a smile from the old man as he realized his field days were over.

But that smile didn't last long.

"Get your ass back into the fight, Duffy. If you see a medic, send him over if he ain't too busy. And find your own damned rifle."

I did what I was told, all except for the rifle thing. There wasn't a snowball's chance in hell I was going back into battle with my piece of shit. And I took all of his ammo too.

The reinforcements moved the gooks back and we were following. My ankle didn't seem so bad after I saw the holes in the sarge but it still let me know I wasn't going to be doing any running. I was doing my best to catch up with our guys when a strange feeling came over me. The air was full of shooting and shouting and screaming and exploding shit but I could barely hear it. I even put the pain radiating from my ankle out of my mind temporarily. I'd never seen anything like this but somehow I was feeling very calm. I wondered if the feeling would get me killed. As the battle continued to rage all around me, everything seemed to slow down. In front of me, a lieutenant was trying to move his men forward. They didn't seem very excited to do so as they cowered behind some fallen trees.

"What's the plan, LT?" I shouted.

"We gotta kill that machine gun," he said, pointing to a stand of brush and palm about seventy-five meters out. "That gun has Charlie Company pinned down."

Every ten or so seconds, the gun would send a burst, but it was barely visible as it was hidden in the foliage. It didn't seem to be shooting our way so I got up and grabbed the nearest GI by the collar.

"Follow me!" I screamed, wondering whose voice that was.

We started out laterally, trying to get around the flank. I stole a glance behind me to make sure my ass wasn't hanging out there alone and strangely, there were four guys following me. We kept moving to the right, planning to get around behind the gun and take it out. The LT must have figured out what I was trying to do and he started directing M-79 grenade fire toward the gun. The grenades detonated in trees way before they got to the machine gun position but they did the job of slowing the gun's rate of fire. I'd left the sarge in a slight depression in the jungle floor. That little gully ran along the route we were moving now providing little, but at least some, cover.

"Please God, don't let this goddamned rifle jam on me now," I mumbled.

We saw the bad guys before they saw us and we squeezed first, dropping four guys with ten shots. Round one for the good guys. We were moving way too fast into unknown territory, but that machine gun was doing too much damage to our guys for us to take our time. I don't know what made the other guys follow me. Maybe they thought I knew what I was doing. Maybe they knew what they should be doing or maybe they were just too scared to be cowards. Whatever it was, it got us pretty close to the rattling of the machine gun–or more accurately, machine guns. We could hear one zipping rounds across the jungle floor. But then we heard a heavier sound coming from above us. Shit, I thought, two guns mean two gun teams and we've got four guys. The heavy gun started rattling as we hunkered down in the gully. The guys were bunched around me now, looking every bit as scared as I felt.

"What now?" one of them asked. What now, indeed, I thought.

I looked over the edge of the gulley but all I saw was green. We could hear the guns though, and they didn't sound that far off. I pointed to two of the guys.

"You two move down the gulley a little and throw some frags toward the sound of the guns. Throw 'em high and maybe we get an air burst and scare them into doing something stupid."

The two men slithered down the depression and a minute later I heard the safety pins popping off grenades. Me and the guy with me covered our heads and the explosions sent shrapnel and debris flying all over the place. I motioned to my new friend to follow me forward and we low crawled out. The grenades did something because we heard the other two GIs open up with their M-16s. We didn't know what they were shooting at but I didn't really care either as long as it wasn't at us.

We made it a few more meters when I saw what looked like a pith helmet through the brush. I pointed it out to my guy and sighted just like they taught me in basic training. I took a breath and squeezed. The pith helmet flew back into the jungle and we heard the rustling of the brush and some whispered Vietnamese. I got on my knees and flipped the rifle to full automatic and sprayed the rest of the magazine into the brush. I was reloading and listening to some more Vietnamese shouting when M-16 fire from our right exploded. We inched forward some more and got our first look at the machine gun. It rested on bipod legs and pointed from under a redoubt of logs and dirt. One body was all we saw and it looked like he was asleep. We got a little bolder and stood to see where the other gun was. Some more rifle fire to our right erupted. The other GIs were popping targets scattered by the grenades. Then the jungle blew up around us. Branches were chopped off the trees. Dirt coughed up in big chunks of brown. One of our guys must have fired an anti-tank rocket at the sound of the guns. He missed and the noise of a heavy machine gun cranked up again. We fell instinctively, with the big bullets zipping overhead.

"You got 'em?" I shouted.

"Fuck no I ain't got 'em," was the answer as the jungle echoed with more firing.

I was thinking of our next move when some screaming and shooting came from our right. Our two buddies got a bead on the machine gun when he opened fire on us and assaulted from behind it. It was like John Wayne and Audie Murphy came flying to our rescue. They were shooting and screaming and acting all kinds of crazy. When one gook fell from the tree, we got the message and started shooting too. When we stopped to reload, everything was quiet.

"Cease fire, you crazy bastards!" I shouted but they continued to pepper the trees with rifle fire. "Cease fire!" I yelled again and this time they stopped.

"Thanks," I said when they came into view.

"Thanks, shit. We only stopped because we're out of ammo. How many of those motherfuckers did we get?"

"I don't know but if we don't let the rest of our guys know where we are, we might be the next motherfuckers who get got. We ain't got a radio so someone start waving at them before they blow our shit away."

That pretty much ended the fight. Some helicopter gunships got in the action a little later as they caught the bad guys trying to make it across some paddies to get to deeper woods on the other side and all in all, it was a good day for us–as long as "us" wasn't Charlie Company. The ambush killed eleven and wound sixteen before we were able to reinforce.

We were trying to chop some room for the birds to land and ferry out the wounded and the dead. I was included in the former, my ankle as fucked up as it was. While we were waiting, the lieutenant chewed my ass out for being dumb enough to forward without a radio.

"There's a big difference between reckless and brave," he said, "and you'd better learn the difference before we're putting you in a bag, Duffy. So knock that shit off!"

"What shit would that be, sir, saving the company's ass?"

I smiled. He didn't.

CHAPTER FIVE

PIN THE MEDAL ON THE DONKEY

I got two days in the hospital to heal my screwed up ankle. In the midst of my basking in the paradise of air conditioning, cool white sheets, American nurses and three hot meals everyday, the lieutenant showed up to rain on my parade.

"The good news is that you got promoted to sergeant," he told me. "The bad news is that you are now the first squad leader."

"Bullshit, LT, this is a terrible mistake," I said. "I have a hard enough time taking care of myself much less a whole squad. You really can't do this."

"Quiet down, Duffy," the lieutenant responded. "I really can and I really did. It's done. You are the new squad leader. The sarge is on his way home with a million-dollar wound. And for some strange reason, he thought you should be the guy to take his place."

"Christ, LT, Sargent York couldn't take his place."

"I know, Duffy, but all we have is you."

That was two weeks ago and so far, so good. We had a cake job guarding a Montagnard village. Now all we had to do was pull some night patrols around the village and set up some night ambushes waiting for what we prayed would not happen. And one of the guys must have had a way to be heard by the Big Guy upstairs because our efforts resulted only in some lost sleep.

We were sitting in the shade when she sauntered by.

The late afternoon sun cast the long-limbed, lithe woman in an alluring shade of bronze as she ambled down the path in her tightly wrapped sarong. The sway of her hips matched the jiggle of her bare breasts as she balanced a big water jug on her head. No one said a word. We just stared at the bounce of her boobs and the taut nipples centered on her golden breasts.

"Look, but don't even think about touching," I said.

"You got that right," the radioman added. "I heard about a dude in Charlie Company who thought he might leave a few fingerprints on such fine Montagnard titties, and ain't nobody heard from him again. He just up and gone."

"He's probably in a few pieces feeding tigers and

whatever else is out there," I said, looking toward the jungle. "That's why I have my special lady here with me all the time.

"She never complains. She's always ready. And no chance of losing a limb because somebody got jealous." I stroked the fluffy gray fur hanging from my rucksack.

"That was pure genius, Duffy, turning these leather gloves inside out," the machine gun guy said. "That fur feels so goddamned good when I'm stroking."

"Sure beats the hell out of sloppy fourths and fifths," the radioman said.

A dozen rucksacks were strewn around the bunker and a furry leather glove was a prominent feature on most. But all eyes in the squad were focused on the woman's butt as she undulated down the path toward the well. The radioman took a long drink of warm Pepsi.

"It don't get much better than this," he said.

"It sure don't," I said. "But it ain't going to last. You can count on that so enjoy it while you can. Just remember the Montagnard men are real particular about protecting their women."

The little new guy from Tennessee laughed his nervous, high-pitched laugh. I don't think the kid hit puberty yet. He was the only one lacking a glove on his ruck. He hadn't been with us long enough to appreciate the joy of leather and fur.

"This here is like watching a Playboy magazine instead of reading one," he said.

"Read, kid? You know you can't read a lick," I said and everyone else laughed, even the ones who couldn't read themselves.

Rather than get into education the kid changed the subject.

"What's with them leather gloves, y'all? It's hotter than Tennessee tar in July and you got leather gloves. I think y'all are crazy."

"Weather ain't the only concern around here, boy," the machine gun guy said. "Some other important things have to be taken care of too."

"Hell, yeah," the radioman said. "Cold ain't nothing compared to lonely."

The squad was laughing pretty hard now, and that made the kid a little pissed off.

"Should I sell him my extra glove, Sarge?" the radioman said.

"Hell, no," I said. "At the rate you're beating your meat, you'll need the other glove any time now." Now the squad was laughing hysterically and the kid thought we were making fun of him. I didn't want to see the kid make a scene so I gave him an explanation of the glove syndrome.

"When I first came over here, kid, I was a virgin. I lost my cherry in a whorehouse a long way from here. But the little whore was so ugly and the experience so nasty, I decided I'd never do that shit again."

I was going to go on but the kid looked confused.

"Where did I lose you, son?"

"Beat his meat, Sarge, what's that?"

"You know, he pounded his pud, choked his chicken, strangled his pants python ..."

"Oh, he jerked off," the kid said. "Why didn't you just say so?"

The radioman laughed so hard he had Pepsi coming out his nose, giving the squad sights and sounds to laugh at.

"The kid is familiar with the concept, Sarge, not the terminology," the machine gun guy said. "Please continue."

So I did.

"My buddy back home used to brag about all the new ways he'd found to jerk off and we loved hearing his stories, but one thing stuck in my mind and became a real option when I found out how much I despised hookers. He told me he used to take fur-lined leather gloves and turn them inside out and beat off with the fur. So I asked my mother to send me some leather gloves with fur lining because it got cold at night here. And when they got here, I found out my buddy didn't tell no lie. The feel of that fur on my little guy was a feeling that made me swear off whores for the rest of my tour."

The kid looked embarrassed as he lowered his eyes and played with his bootlaces.

"The man speaks the truth, kid," the machine gun guy said. "Once you feel that fur you know what pleasure is."

"So, kid, there is only one question left for you," I said. "Are you right- or left-handed?"

"I'm a righty," Sarge," he said.

The machine gun guy reached in his pack and pulled out a glove.

"We're a match, kid. I'm a lefty."

He threw the glove to the kid and officially made him one of us. But the sight of GIs laughing and having the least bit of fun was enough to drive officers crazy. So it didn't take long for our laughter to gain the attention of the lieutenant who came along looking gaunt and tired.

"Hey LT, you look tired," I said. "You getting enough sleep? You need a vacation? This whole being a leader of men thing looks like it's kicking your young ass."

The guys barely contained their snickering as the lieutenant unfolded a map and spread it on the sandbags.

"You're a real fucking comedian, Duffy," he said without expression. He pointed to a scraggly blue line on the map.

"Take your squad north through the village and patrol up to this creek. Let's make sure this area is as pacified as it is supposed to be."

"Roger that," I said. "We'll push off in five."

As the officer moved away the bitching started.

"How come we always get picked to do this shit," the radioman said. "It's always got to be us."

"It's like that flower delivery service says: when you care enough to send the very best." I said. "So let's cut the bullshit and get it done."

"What are we doing in this ville anyway, Sarge?" the machine gun guy asked. "We ain't seen nothing but old men and half-naked women."

"There's more to this village than naked tits, guys," I said. "The reason you don't see any younger guys is because they are mercenaries out with the Green Berets chasing the VC. We don't want anything happening to the villagers while the men are out helping Americans, do we?"

A few minutes later, we were moving down the dusty trail into the Montagnard village. They derived their name – mountain people -- from the French colonial period. While the ethnic Vietnamese could trace their roots to China, the Montagnards were much darker skinned and their women walked around bare-breasted and the little boys never wore pants. The women could make Vietnam almost beautiful.

✓The Montagnards were a valuable asset to the Americans because of their hatred of the Viet Cong and their incredible tracking skills. About forty thousand 'Yards fought alongside American forces. That led to their merciless persecution once the communists took over the country.)

We moved into the village where thatched huts were perched atop ten-foot stilts to elevate the homes off the jungle floor. Cooking fires and the pungent scent of nouc mam cham carried on the afternoon air. Nouc mam cham was a native hot sauce made from the fermentation of fish entrails. The manufacturing process sounded bad but it was still better than the stuff smelled. At the far end of the ville, larger fires were blazing and the old men were working in the shade, hammering and shaping fine brass and bronze rings and bracelets. I was struck by the contrast between the primitive surroundings and the elegance of the jewelry I saw gleaming on wooden benches. I took a minute to look at the wares and smiled at a weathered old man who stared back at me. The old man's face was almost mahogany in color and deeply lined. His mouth was sprinkled with the gold teeth that were almost indigenous to Vietnam. From his pointed chin, a couple of long white hairs gave him the appearance of an old billy goat. I felt a need to help him but I didn't think patrolling and killing other Vietnamese would do the trick. So I found another way.

"How much, papa-san?" I asked, pointing to

delicately shaped bronze band.

The old man held up four fingers. I held up two. He split the difference and we settled on three dollars. I laughed a little to myself, knowing that had I asked him anything about anything, he would have merely given me that puzzled "I speak no English" look. But talk about money and he knew exactly what I was saying. I found a couple of American dollars I was hanging onto and gave them to the old man. His eyes sparkled a bit at the sight of the American money and he bowed politely. He put the thin band on my little finger and I returned the bow and moved out. We still had a patrol to run.

Two hours later, we returned to the bunkers on the outskirts of the village. I was soaked through with sweat and the coolness of the shade in the gathering dusk felt good. The lieutenant came over.

"How did it go out there, Duffy?"

"If we had clubs, LT, we could have played 18. It was a walk in the park."

The lieutenant smiled and moved on. I hung my shirt on a pole to dry and took the leather glove off my rucksack. I took the ring off my little finger when the radioman came over.

"What are you doing, Sarge?"

"I'm going to make an honest woman out of my

glove, my friend," and I slid the ring over the third finger of the glove.

The radioman's face wrinkled up in a half-frown, half-grin.

"You are one crazy sumbitch. Let me see that."

He looked at my glove and laughed.

"Where the hell did you get that?"

"The old man near the end of the village path. He had a lot of cool shit."

We babysat the Montagnard village for almost two weeks. It gave us a much-needed break from the war as we sat around at night telling the semi-true stories of life back in the World. And it gave my aching ankle a few more days to heal. We read and wrote letters. We had hot chow twice and ate some interesting native food. No one tried to mate with a Montagnard woman so we all kept our balls in pairs, and the old man pounding out jewelry in the ville did a brisk business as my squad got hitched to their gloves. But all good things come to an end and too soon. We were packing up for the march back in to the jaws of the jungle when I saw the lieutenant approach.

"Sergeant Duffy, the captain wants to see you." It's always bad when they use your rank.

"Fuck, LT, I didn't do anything wrong did I? What

does he want with me?"

"I'm not sure but I think it's something good. Something to do with all the commercial activity in the village while we were here."

"Shit, what does that have to do with me? We were just having a little fun."

As we walked to the captain's bunker, I thought about all the times I screwed the pooch by "having fun." I was still searching the recesses of my mind for what I might have done to deserve face time with the commanding officer when I snapped to attention in front of the field table that served as his desk.

"At ease, sergeant," the captain said. "Well, you've really done it this time, Duffy."

"I don't suppose the Fifth Amendment still applies in a combat zone, sir?" I never missed an opportunity to try to jam some verbiage up the captain's tight ass.

"Can the bullshit, Duffy. I am not impressed by your supposed wit. This is going to be hard enough as it is.

"It seems that the brain trust back at brigade has heard about the increased levels of economic activity here in the village that indicate a dramatic rise in the personal income of several of the craftsmen since the arrival of Delta Company and particularly stimulated by the first platoon."

Thinking better of it all the while, I couldn't help but

respond.

"You mean we bought a lot of stuff from the 'Yards," I said, using the GI vernacular for Montagnards.

Even the lieutenant saw the humor in that and was losing the battle not to show it. That didn't make the captain any happier.

"Knock it off, Duffy!" the captain snapped. "You know goddamned well what I mean. This all plays into the hearts and minds bullshit that is so important in the rear, so they checked it out and it appears they've traced a good bit of the activity to your squad.

"So just to prove that medals occasionally pin themselves on donkeys, the battalion commander is coming out in about thirty minutes to present you with the Army Commendation Medal."

That must have truly rubbed the captain the wrong way. He was a pompous ass through and through and seeing anyone flaunt the precious army regulations and be recognized for it would surely piss him off. I should have let it go at that but I couldn't let the moment pass without rubbing his nose in it a little more.

"My mom and dad will be very proud, sir."

The captain turned quickly to the lieutenant.

"Get him cleaned up! Let's get this nonsense over with so we can get back in the jungle where we belong."

"Roger that, sir," the lieutenant said, grabbing my elbow and ushering me out of the bunker before I could incite the captain further.

Forty-three minutes later, the battalion commander stood before the men of first platoon and pinned the medal with its green and white ribbon on me as the division executive officer read from my citation: "In recognition of the understanding and appreciation of the plight of the indigenous population of the Republic of Vietnam and for taking initiative at the infantry squad level to invigorate the local economy through the involvement of American troops in domestic industry purchases ..." blah, blah, blah.

As the lieutenant colonel shook my hand he kept glancing at my glove hanging from my rucksack. I couldn't hide the smile and neither could the rest of the guys even they held their collective breath waiting for the inevitable question.

"Fur gloves, Sergeant Duffy? A little unusual, isn't it?"

"Well sir, it can get cool in the evenings up here and you know what they say about cold hands and warm hearts."

"Indeed. Well, son, carry on. You are doing an outstanding job."

I just grinned and saluted.

The commander's chopper was winging its way back

to his air-conditioned trailer when the radioman took my citation from my hands.

"You know what this says, right Duffy? It is a bunch of fancy bullshit saying you got a medal for jerking off."

"Yeah, ain't it grand?" I said, thinking I finally found a match between what the Army likes and what I do best. Maybe my luck was finally changing. But it wasn't.

CHAPTER SIX

THE CHASE

After our semi-successful stint in the Montagnard village, we were shuttled around our area of operation like pins on a map—which is exactly what we were to the big thinkers in their air-conditioned trailers far from the consequences of their decisions. I asked about getting frequent flier miles from all our trips but the lieutenant didn't think I was very funny.

But today there was nothing funny about our situation. The molten heat of the sun scorched the color from the sky. It spread over us with a suffocating heat that made every step an ordeal. The landscape shimmered like it was under a layer of glass. Even breathing was a pain in the ass. The hot air that I sucked into my nostrils bristled against the nose hairs and tingled the membranes with stinging heat. Sweat roiled under my steel pot and streamed down my face in salty rivers that clouded my vision and rolled into my mouth, making me even thirstier. My brain must have reached the limit of its tolerance as it commanded my mouth to start uttering whispered prayers that I might get shot.

"Sweet Jesus, don't make me move another step in this inferno. Give me a bullet in the leg or the arm or in my ass. Hell, shoot me in the face if I can stop moving in this hellacious heat."

But God must have busy again that day so nothing happened. On we trudged, our shuffling steps kicking up little clouds of dust under the molten glare of the sun. My mouth was stuck in the open position as I tried to suck in as much oxygen as I could but it felt like I was breathing in a furnace.

We'd been patrolling a place that a French writer once called "the street without joy." He got that right. There was no shade for miles nor was there a "street." We walked astride a cow path that might have been passable for an ox cart but little else. Every now and then, we'd happen on a concrete bunker left by the ill-fated French who fought and died there. But there was little else under this punishing sun. Each minute I walked reminded me that we weren't the first to suffer here. That thought and the heat burned into my psyche like hot coals.

But now, we'd moved to the east, in the direction of the South China Sea. At least, that's what my map said. But the sea and the water in it were only rumors from where we stood. The only things that held water were our canteens and there wasn't a whole lot in them either.

Our path turned and we headed toward what might have once been a hamlet. There were a few walls where huts might have been, some overgrown paths, and what looked like a well. I sent the point man to check it out but it was as dry and barren as everything else. A hundred meters ahead was our objective—a bombed out church that was thought to harbor bad guys. I thought that the big brains in the rear might have thought a few jets screaming over the ruins with some high explosive bombs and napalm might have accomplished in seconds what we were trying to do in hours but what did I know?

We encountered a little shade thrown by some banana trees and some other stunted trees struggling to grow in the absence of water. As we moved closer to the church, I could see bullet holes and explosion pockets that had caricatured a face into the wall and it rose over the ghost ville like a sinister frown. I held up the patrol and took some water from my canteen to wash the sweat out of my eyes. The radioman approached.

"Hey Sarge, the Six is on the horn and wants to know when we will be starting back."

The captain was perched on the only high ground for miles and had a pretty good view of the squad's progress.

"Fuck me," I said. "The asshole sends us out here in this fucking heat on this bullshit patrol and now he wants to know when we'll be back? Does he miss me or what?"

"Should I ask him?" the radioman said with a smile.

I took the handset.

"Six, this is one-one, go."

"That's a good idea, Duffy. Why don't you 'go' and get this over with?"

"The church is just ahead and I'm sending some guys to reconnoiter, over.

"I've seen men walk faster than you going to the gas chamber," the captain said. "Get the recon done, the quicker you can get your butts back here."

I released the push-to-talk button.

"Yeah, and the quicker you can kiss my salt stained ass, you sorry piece of dog shit."

I turned to the men spread out under any hint of shade they could find.

"On your feet, troops! Six is watching us and thinks we're fucking the dog so let's get the recon over and start back."

The guys grumbled as they stood, cursing the order that brought them here and now questioned their progress. It was nice to know that I wasn't the only one who thought the captain was an asshole. But that wasn't the issue here. I called up the team leaders.

"Take this nice and slow, kiddies. Alpha team, go around the right flank and Bravo, you have the left. Me and the radio and doc go up the middle to coordinate. Keep me in sight and watch my hand signals."

Both team leaders looked at me through flat, glassy eyes and nodded blankly. I didn't like this at all. The guys were beat to shit and were just about wrung out. We'd been prowling through the heat that was as thick as peanut butter and a lot of them were on the edge of exhaustion. Tired soldiers were careless soldiers. But orders were orders, even when they didn't make much sense. The frowning wall stared at me like a warning as the teams headed for the flanks.

The radioman was a few steps behind me.

"You know, once upon a time," I said, "I hitchhiked for two days and nights just to find the sun in Florida. Somehow, this sun doesn't seem the same."

"I never did understand you white folk, laying out in the hot sun," the radioman replied. "Y'all jest crazy, man."

The bullet that smacked into the point man's flesh

sounded like a bag of water dropped from a second story window. It knocked him back and the jangle of his rifle and helmet were the next sounds I heard. By the time I turned around the doc was already applying pressure to the wound with a bandage.

I grabbed the handset.

"Six, this one-one, we are taking fire from the church... repeat rounds from the church... one friendly down... we need fire support now!"

"One-one, this is Six India ... affirmative on the fire support ... we've got our tube ready and the first shot is out... get your asses down, over!"

The shrieking whistle of the mortar rounds provided a little reassurance as I checked the pointman's leg. The bullet had driven into the outside part of his leg and tore a chunk of meat off. The doc was skillfully applying a tourniquet to stem the flow of blood. Even hearing him moaning in pain, I was envious.

Why the fuck couldn't I get one and get out of this hellhole?

The thump and crack of the mortar rounds impacting around the ruined church snapped me out of illusions of what might have been. I grabbed the handset again and started giving the gunners corrections.

"Six India, this is one-one ... add five zero meters and

move left two-five meters and fire for effect!"

The air came alive with the whirring and whizzing of the mortar rounds flaying through the heat on the way to the target. The screaming of the shells was a symphony to the boys and me. We were hunkered down behind whatever cover we could find and looked for anything even remotely resembling the enemy.

The frowning wall groaned and wobbled under the impact of the mortar shells before it collapsed into dust.

"Six India, cease fire! We're going in!"

The dust was still rising as I started the charge. The rest of the squad took their flanks and followed. We were just twenty meters from the church when a machine gun opened up on us. A round tore off a banana frond near my head but I could see where the shots came from.

"Machine gun! You got that motherfucker? He's under the overhang near the front of the church!"

The rattle of our M-60 answered that question as bullets rattled across the front of the building. The enemy gun stopped and as I got closer, I saw the shooter's body draped over the gun.

But my guy didn't get hit by a machine gun round, I thought, as we moved in a straight line of wary men into the rubble of the church. Someone is still in here wanting to shoot me.

Off to my right, a single shot rang out and was followed by the cry "another one down!" I stepped over some broken concrete when I heard the machine gun guy.

"Down Duffy!"

I dropped and a single round smacked into the broken wall behind me. The remains of the church poked and jabbed and jutted into me but it still felt like safety to me. I poked my head up in time to see a guy jump out of a palm tree and start running.

"This motherfucker is mine," I yelled, taking off after the VC who was running east, toward the sea.

Think you're going to swim for it? I thought, as I sprinted across the flat ground. I got rid of my helmet and ignored the heat as I ran after the man who tried to kill me. I was fueled by equal parts adrenalin and the energy of hatred. A few minutes into the run, the heat reminded me where I was and I wondered if this was really worth it. The sweat was boiling off me in waves and my eyes stung while my breath got more labored. But I heard the shouts of the guys behind me and I kept after my prey.

Who's going to quit first? I wondered, breathing with lungs on fire.

The bad guy had about fifty meters on me and I thought if I lost any more ground ahead, I'd let him go.

We'd run about a half-mile when the sand flat turned

into a latticework of rice paddies. The three-foot dikes
would be a bigger problem for his short legs than mine.
I knew then I could catch him. I was running on fumes
when the sniper threw his rifle away. I took a dike with a
single stride and splashed through the cow shit floating in
the paddy. The VC was climbing over the dikes while I
was taking them like hurdles. The distance closed and kept
closing. I put my head down to get over a dike and when I
looked up again, the little bastard was gone.

I quick-timed through another paddy scanning ahead
of me but not seeing anything out of the ordinary.

"Where the fuck did you go, Nguyen? " I said out
loud

I made it to another dike when I found out. The sniper
popped out of the water, his breath exploding from him in
a loud shout. I was frozen as I watched him lob a grenade
toward me. Tired, pissed off, and caught unaware, I was
going to die in this shitty rice paddy. I heard the ping of the
safety as it popped off the grenade. I watched it arc over my
head. The fuse was supposed to blast the little bomb in four
seconds. I counted to three and waited for the explosion
that would surely kill me. But the only sound I heard was
a splash in the muddy water behind me. I'm not ashamed
to say I pissed myself somewhere around the count of two.
But it was a dud. I was saved because some asshole in some

factory had done a piss poor job of creating lethality.

Then I saw the sniper's hand shoot up in the air.

"Chieu Hoi!" he shouted, indicating his defeat. "Chieu Hoi!" *Now*, the little bastard wanted to surrender. He was unarmed and I was good and pissed so it seemed like a good time for him to cut his losses.

"Oh sure," I said. "What a great time to surrender, you little fuck. You wanted to blow my fucking head off but now it's time to give up?"

I could tell he didn't understand a word I was saying but I really didn't care. English was going to be the last language this fucker heard. The time to surrender had come and gone. I had a little respect for the prick before he put his hands up. But now, wet with my own piss, winded by this stupid chase, and still shaking with fear, I hated this sonofabitch with all the hate I could muster.

The VC kept repeating the words of surrender and bowing like that might make me forget he tried to kill me. I smiled at him as I moved forward until I was close enough to snatch his hair. In a single motion I yanked his head back and jammed my rifle into his mouth.

"Chieu Hoi, my ass" I said, still smiling as I pulled the trigger. The bullet shot out the back of the sniper's head and went right through my fingers. I forgot to let go before I shot. I let him fall into the paddy and watched his blood mix with the muddy water.

I felt an arm wrap around me and saw big hand attached to it and knew it was the machine gun guy.

"You OK, Sarge. You took care of business. You OK, bro."

But I knew that wasn't true. I wasn't OK, not by a long shot. My fingers were seared but that pain was nothing compared to the ache in my soul. What had I become? What was left for me after this? What would I be tomorrow?

I dropped to a knee, partly from exhaustion and mostly from the knowledge that I'd been defeated. I'd completely lost my way. I'd lost my soul. My ears kept hearing the machine gun guy telling me I was OK, and I knew there was no point in trying to tell him why he was wrong. I had lost a bigger part of me than if that grenade had actually exploded.

CHAPTER SEVEN

THE FACE OF AN ANGEL

"Telly? What the fuck kind of name is Telly?" I asked. "You named after that bald-headed actor who was in 'The Dirty Dozen'?"

"No, Sarge, Telly is a warrior name," he said. "I am named after Telemachus, a great Greek fighter in our mythology."

"So, are you a warrior, Telly?"

"I want to be, sir."

"I'm not a 'sir.' I'm a sergeant, kid. Remember that."

The kid had the face of an angel but he was named after some kind of Greek hero. I don't think he had the need to shave that baby face yet and he looked pretty silly with the steel helmet that dwarfed his head.

But those were the kind of kids we were getting as

replacements. The war was getting hotter with each passing month and more old hands needed replacing. So we'd get a kid like this, right out of advanced training, to take the place of a troop who'd been in the boondocks for a few months and was starting to know its way around. We were taking two steps forward and three back.

Warrior? I thought, this kid doesn't look strong enough to punch his way out of a jelly donut. The kid looked more like the angels I'd seen painted on the ceiling of my church back in the World.

"How old are you Telly?" I asked.

"Almost 19, Sarge."

"How 'almost?'"

Well, in nine months I'll be 19."

What the fuck? I wondered. They keep sending these young kids into this shit. Why don't they at least wait until they can shave?

"How long you been in-country, Telly?"

"Almost a month."

"Where have you been for almost a month?"

"I was over in Bravo Company but they said Delta needed some replacements so they sent me over here."

"You weren't a fuck-up, were you, Telly? 'Cuz they usually don't send their best troops to someone else as replacements."

"No, Sarge, I did good over there, honest."

I doubted that but I had no say in the matter. When you said you needed bodies, they sent you bodies but no company wanted to part with its solid soldiers.

We'd been out in the jungle for only two weeks when they called us in for a stand down. The second night I figured this piece-of-cake listening post would be a pretty good way to measure my little Greek warrior's skills.

"Drop your duffle bag over at supply and then come over to the squad area for the mission brief for tonight. We've got the LP out to the east side of the base tonight."

"Yessir, Sarge."

I hope you can soldier, I thought as the kid hustled off. I got the feeling we're going to need some good troops.

Late in the afternoon, I headed to a bunker to sit in the dark for a while so my night vision would kick in. I wasn't worried about the mission. We needed to go out only about a thousand meters, sit our asses down, and wait for something we hoped wouldn't come our way. I closed my eyes and took a little nap before it was time to go.

My radioman came in to wake me before I got Raquel Welch's dress off in my dream. Somebody always woke me before I did. I climbed out of the hole in the ground that was the bunker. It was dark.

"Where's the squad?" I asked.

"The team leaders are bringing them over but I think we got us a problem."

"And what might that problem be?"

"I think our new guy is wasted," the radioman said. "He hooked up with those two surfer dudes from California and they introduced his young ass to pot."

"Fuck! I need bodies out there tonight. Get the three assholes over here!"

A few minutes later, the three guys were standing in front of me. Two of them looked OK but my Greek warrior had eyes that looked like two piss holes in the snow.

"What the fuck are you douche bags thinking?" I asked. "We're heading out in thirty minutes and you dicks are stoned."

"No, Sarge, we ain't even stoned," one of the dudes said. "We took a few tokes but we'll be all right."

"What about you, Greek warrior? You all right to go outside the wire tonight?"

"Hell yeah, Sarge. I'm feeling good."

I got the team leaders together and told them I wanted to take the two stoners but leave the new guy behind.

"You do that, Sarge, and the kid gets court-martialed and sent to the stockade. Kid like him would get eaten alive in there."

"Well, what the fuck am I going to do with him? He

looks worse than I did after a weekend bender."

"I'll get the two surfers to keep an eye on him," the machine gunner said. "They look OK, right?"

"Yeah but I should throw *their* asses in jail for being so fucking stupid."

"Hey, Sarge, don't sweat it. A little pot is like a couple of beers. The guys will be cool. I'll tell them we'll kick their asses if anything happens."

Fuck, I thought. My Greek going to jail would not have been pretty. I don't want these guys thinking they can get away with this shit but what am I going to do with this kid?

"Get the three brain surgeons over here," I said. Not long after, the three stoners were standing in front of me. Two of them didn't look bad. The kid was a little wobbly.

"Here's the choices we got, assholes," I said. "I send young Telly here over to battalion with an escort and the next time anyone hears about him, he'll be in Long Binh Jail.

"Or you two can clean up the shit you dropped by taking the kid with us and watching him so nothing happens. What's it going to be?"

"Hell, Sarge, we ain't even high," one of the stoners said. "We can take care of him. But you don't want to be sending him to jail, do you?"

"Fuck, no I don't but you might have noticed during the last few weeks that we are fighting a war, not fucking around here. I need you two assholes to take care of the kid tonight and I'll figure out what to do with the three of you later. You dig?"

"Hell yeah, Sarge, we're on it. He's in our hands."

Somehow their assent didn't exactly fill me with confidence. But we had a job to do and do it we would. I went down the line and checked everyone out before we headed out. Ten minutes later we were at the barbed wire and moving out to find our spot. We were tasked with keeping an eye on a trail that led to a Buddhist monastery. There had been a report that the VC were sneaking around at night and hiding out in the monastery. It sounded like all the other bullshit missions we were given; it was based on a rumor rather than fact. Someone told someone who told someone else who gave us the mission to listen and observe. Very little ever resulted from these little excursions except that we lost a lot of sleep we couldn't afford to lose.

We moved like a long, slithering snake across open ground and into a thinly wooded area. We had to go a hundred meters or so to the farthest edge of the tree line where we could get a clear line of sight to a trail that led to the monastery. But first, we had to disguise our movement, continuing past the woods and looping around in the dark to come back to our spot. Everything was going smoothly so I started to think my stoners were OK.

Our listening post was along a low rise that looked like an old rice paddy dike. I'd been out in this area before and I knew that this would provide some cover and concealment. We circled around in a wide pattern then headed back to the woods. We moved well in the darkness and the brush making little noise. We reached the edge of the dike looking out to the trail that was about fifty meters in front of us. I moved along the squad setting my teams. I put the stoners about five meters from the machine gun. Then we settled in to wait; wait for the VC to come along or the nearing of dawn, which would be our cue to head back to the base.

I sat with my back to the dike giving my back a little relief from all the shit that it had been made to carry. I took a drink from my canteen. Some of the water fell on to my fingers, mingling with the filth that accumulates in the jungle. I rubbed my thumb and forefinger together and balled up the dirt so I could flick it into the brush. Times like this were a two-edged sword. We got a little rest, if not sleep, while we were on these jaunts. These missions served to remind us how beaten down physically we'd become. They gave us a little recharge.

But it also gave me too much time to think, to muse

about the twisted, gnarled path my life had taken to get me to this time in this place. It gave me time to mourn the lost months this war was taking from me. But most of all, it gave me too much time to remember who I was and what I was becoming.

I turned my attention to the trail and the mission. It was a good night: no moon but lots of stars. We might be in the asshole of the world but you could see every star in the sky and they were beautiful.

It was zero three hundred and I had just called in to tell the base everything was normal when it suddenly turned abnormal. The M-60 opened up with a burst and some rifle fire followed. I looked out at the trail but saw nothing.

"Cease fire!" I screamed. "Cease fire! What are we shooting at?"

It took a few seconds but the shooting stopped. I scurried down to the machine position.

"What the fuck are you shooting at?"

"There was movement out about twenty meters, Sarge. I saw it clear as shit."

I saw nothing moving anywhere.

"You two, get out there and see what we shot up," I whispered. I saw the fear on their faces.

"All right, you come with me if you need me to hold your fucking hands."

And out we went, over the low dike and toward the trail. My two amigos were trailing behind me when I saw the body. Using hands signals, I moved them to my right and left as I crept forward.

Let's see what the fuck we've got, I thought, as I inched my way up. When I could see, I wanted to throw up. There, staring up at me with that angelic face was my Greek warrior, his body riddled with bullets. I knelt down and looked at him one more time. His zipper was open so I wondered if he had to piss and walked out in front of our listening post. It didn't make any difference though. Why this happened didn't make much difference. He was still dead and we were still the ones who killed him.

I picked up his body and hoisted him on to my shoulder. His blood was still leaking and I could feel it running down my chest. I could also feel the burning hatred mounting in me for my role in killing this kid. I wanted to be a nice guy, to do the "right" thing and that got this kid killed. I also knew that two other assholes shared the blame--two other dickheads who were supposed to watch the kid. As I stumbled back to the listening post, I resolved to kill both of them.

"Sarge, I ain't never seen you carrying no dead gook," the radioman said.

"He ain't a dead gook. He's a dead GI."

I laid the kid down behind the dike.

"Call it in as hostile action, a hit-and-run job," I told the radioman. "Tell them we have one KIA and possibly two more."

"Roger that, Sarge."

I went down the line to find my two stoners. Both were huddled with the machine gun guy who must have sensed my intention. He stood over me and whispered.

"Not here and not now, Duffy. You can't grease them in front of all these witnesses. Get them another day, another place."

One of the stoners started to say something. I stopped him.

"I swear to God that if you say one fucking word to me I will kill you on the spot and fuck the consequences. You two cocksuckers got this kid killed. Just like a couple beers you said. Yeah, just like it except nobody drinks a couple of beers before they go out.

"You two pricks better ask for a transfer when we get back 'cuz if you stay with me you will never make it home. Do you understand?"

One of them stood up and I took it as an attempt to challenge me but I didn't wait to find out. My right fist caught him square on the nose and he went down. The blood had started to flow before he hit the ground.

"Sarge," he said through the blood and the pain, "you broke my fucking nose."

"Be thankful that's all he broke," the machine gun guy said. "Now pick up your shit. We're moving out."

"I want you two motherfuckers in front of me at all times," I said. "If you aren't in front of me, I'll kill you both."

The machine gun guy looked at me and then at the two stoners.

"He means it and if he needs a witness to say it was self-defense, he's got one."

I went back to where I'd left the Greek's body. I handed my rifle to the radioman and hefted the kid on to my shoulder again.

"Sarge, you don't need to be carrying the kid," he said.

"Yeah I do. Now let's get back to the base."

We headed back with a lot less stealth than we had when we came out. There was no point in trying to conceal our presence now. As I carried the kid back I almost hoped we'd get hit and that I might get killed to atone for my sin. But the return was uneventful. When we reached the wire, I saw the ambulance waiting to take my new guy.

Just about then, I heard the words of the old sarge echoing in my head.

"Kindness is weakness," he told me. I didn't believe it then but I sure as hell did now. My "kindness" got my Greek warrior killed and that was a mistake I couldn't ever make again.

When we made it through the wire, the lieutenant was waiting for us.

"You hit, Duffy?" he asked, seeing the kid's blood all over me.

"No such luck, LT, my wound ain't bleeding but it's a lot deeper."

He had no idea what I was talking about.

CHAPTER EIGHT

CAN'T WIN; CAN'T QUIT

Now I knew what my mother had meant when she told us "it's raining harder than a cow pissing on a flat rock." She was full of those cute, Texas-inspired axioms that always made me smile. It helped to think of those axioms to remind myself of a time better than this. The monsoon rain hammered a relentless drumbeat on my skull. Memory was a band-aid on nights like this, with my soul as bleak and blackened as the jungle we were prowling through. It was hard to reconcile the extremes of this God-forsaken country. One minute the landscape was a barren brown and walking kicked up choking dust. Then the monsoon would come and everything was turned into a muddy pudding by sheets of rain that fell with more velocity than I'd ever known. We were trapped in a land of absolutes–total darkness or blinding sun … drought or flood … alive or suddenly dead. We were in a land of polar opposites without transitions or gray areas.

Lifting my feet had become too much of a chore with the soup on the jungle floor sucking at my feet. So I just slid them through the slime. The rain didn't just punish me physically. It penetrated my soul with icy fingers that chilled me from the inside out. The darkness made me feel more alone. The rain reminded me of the hopelessness of my situation. The combination made me want to simply quit, to declare myself the loser of this struggle and sit down and pray I'd never have the strength to stand. That kind of thinking could get you dead in a hurry. I'd seen it in one of the new guys who caught a bullet through his bicep. It was a million dollar wound: a one-way ticket home. But the kid let the fear of having been hit overtake him and while he was waiting for the medevac bird, he just died. I battled the temptation to give up every day and I was winning. But tonight the despair was as consuming as the rain. What the hell am I doing here? (I no longer believed in the cause, if I had ever believed or ever knew what the cause really was. I was merely marking time until my sentence in this asylum was completed or that odd, angry shot found me and put an end to everything.) Tonight, I was on remote control, moving my feet rather than standing still because moving my feet made everyone in the squad move. The more we moved, the closer we got to ending this stupid patrol and finding some place dry.

I had moved to the point after two of my guys lost their way in the utter blackness of the storm-swept jungle. I wasn't doing a whole lot better but I always made everyone believe I knew what I was doing. The circumstances dictated whether that was a curse or a blessing. Now I faced a situation where I need to pretend. I held up the advance by raising my hand. I needed to see where this trail was going. Trail walking was never a good idea but in this soup, there was little alternative. I advanced slowly hoping not to get slapped in the face with a wet branch. I knelt to see if the view from below was any better and saw a slight bend to the left. I kept following the trail on my hands and knees and as I went around the bend, I felt the hair on my neck rise up in fear. Not even the rain could dampen my internal radar. Someone was up ahead of me where no one should be. I stopped and flicked the selector switch on my rifle from "safe" to "semi" and I listened. I listened real hard and when I heard a splash, I fired three rounds into the darkness. My fire was returned tenfold with some telltale green tracers lighting the blackness.

Don't use tracers at night, Nguyen, I thought and sent a volley of fire at the source of the tracers.

The next sounds I heard were the splashing of feet and the muffled voices of someone moving away. I waited and I prayed that I was alone again. The radioman came forward.

"You OK, Sarge?" he asked.

"I'm good. Just waiting to see if I hit anything up ahead. I heard some voices and popped off a few rounds."

"Yeah. We saw the tracers coming this way, those pretty green commie tracers. Who the fuck uses tracers on a night as black as this?"

I wondered that too. Tracers let you see where you were shooting, but they also let the enemy know where you were.

"Bring the rest of the guys up," I instructed. "I'm going forward to see what's up there."

The radioman went one way and I went the other. I didn't have to go too far to hear the low moans coming from a shadow ahead of me. I stopped and got my rifle back to the ready and inched ahead. I came on the form of a body leaning up against a tree. As moved closer, I could see he was holding his stomach. He had no visible weapon so I moved even closer. What I could see through the rain was the face of a boy. I didn't even think he was in his teens. He was scared and hurting; both because I shot him. I reached out my hand to touch him and he grabbed my wrist. I used the only Vietnamese I knew.

"GI bic," I said a couple of times, telling him I understood his fear and his pain

I pulled my field dressing from my belt and used it to cover his wound. He was trembling so I gave him a drink from my canteen. He drank from it and returned it to me. His tension eased and he sat up a little straighter. It didn't take long for the rest of the squad to reach my position.

"Spread out and make sure this guy's pals don't come back," I said, and the men moved out into the jungle. "Doc, take a look at this and see what you think?"

"Whoa, Sarge. Is that your field dressing on his wound? You get religion all of sudden or what?"

"Shut the fuck up and see what you can do for this kid."

When he saw I wasn't kidding, the medic went to work. He was putting a bandage here and sticking him with a needle there.

"What did you give him?" I asked. "Is he going to make it?"

"Hard to tell, Sarge. If he lasts the night and we can get a bird in here, he might have a chance. But he's losing a lot of blood. We'll just have to wait and see. I gave him a little morphine to help him with the pain."

I gave the boy another drink from my canteen and settled in beside him.

"How old do you think he is, doc?"

"God, Sarge, he can't be fifteen. He's just a baby-san."

The wounded boy tensed and looked at doc with contempt. The medic tried to make amends.

"Hey kid, I meant no offense. You out here on a shitty night like this, you have to be hard core." The words meant nothing to this kid but the medic's calm voice and delivery appeared soothing.

"See if we can get a chopper in here at first light," I said, and the doc moved off to find the radioman.

I started the normal routine of searching the boy. He tensed again when I touched him but relaxed again when he saw I wasn't going to hurt him. I took out a dozen or so loose rounds for an AK-47, a small notebook, and a couple of rice balls wrapped in wax paper. I broke off a piece of a rice ball and offered it to the boy. He took it and nodded to me. But when I tried to check his chest pocket our truce was in danger. He held my hand tightly when I tried to unbutton his pocket. He finally relented when he saw I wouldn't. I open the pocket and found a black and white photo wrapped in plastic. A pretty, smiling face looked up at me from the picture. I saw the boy looking longingly at the picture and I finally got a smile out of him when I let him hold it. I fed him another ball of rice.

"She number one girl," I said. "Beacoup pretty."

He looked at me and smiled again.

The rain was letting up when the morphine closed the boy's eyes. I stared at him and felt despair crawl through my soul. We'd been thrown together into this stinking, rotten jungle in the midst of a monsoon storm for a hundred seconds of random, mindless violence that wounded us both but in different ways. This kid was suffering from a gunshot wound that might be fixed. I was suffering the death of my soul. I no longer knew who I was but was sure I wasn't the guy who came into this place determined to never kill. A week ago, I was putting bullets into heads to keep the wounded from suffering, now I was despondent over shooting this boy. Who the fuck was I? What was driving me? Could I ever go back to who I was?? Would this madness ever end? Once, I'd thought the death of a friend was worse than killing an enemy. Now, I didn't know who the enemy really was. I didn't even know who I was. Without wanting to, I closed my eyes and slept until I heard the radioman chattering into the handset.

"Roger that, medevac is inbound. We'll be ready."

A smoke grenade was thrown into a clearing nearby. I blinked myself awake.

"Who the fuck let me fall asleep?" I yelled. I stood up to see the boy lying on his side, his eyes frozen in that death stare I had seen way too often. I looked for the medic.

"What happened?" I asked him.

He looked at me with a funny look on his face.

"He died, Sarge. He bled out. There wasn't anything more we could do for him. He just fucking died. There's a lot of that going around right now, in case you hadn't noticed."

I grabbed him by the shirt.

"You going to get smart with me, motherfucker? I know there's a lot of that going around right now and I'm sick of being the asshole spreading it, so fuck you, doc!

"And fuck all the rest of you too!"

I took the barrel of my M-16 and threw the rifle into the jungle.

"That's it! I fucking quit! I'm done! Put me in fucking jail. I don't give a shit. I'm not killing anybody any more!"

Everyone stopped moving or talking. I will forever remember the looks on their faces. They looked like I'd shit in their c-rations. Stunned was the only word I could think to describe them. I put my head in my hands so I couldn't see them.

The machine gunner approached.

"Well now ain't that some shit? You just quit, you say? Just like that? Why 'cuz you killed a kid? That motherfucker would have wasted you in a second, Duffy. He would have blown you away without even thinking 'bout it.

"You beat him to the draw. You did what you were supposed to do and now you feel sorry for yourself."

I stood up to face him.

"So you gonna walk away and hide your head somewhere?" he said. "Well, what about us? You gonna walk away from us too? You gonna leave us out here by ourselves? If you do you ain't shit."

My first impulse was to punch the gunner in the face. I wanted to kick his ass. I wanted to be mad. I wanted to lash out. But I looked around at my squad. I saw their eyes, sunk way back in the skull as if they were in full retreat from the blood and the guts and the gore they saw as regular regimen. Every one of them was a teenager but you could never prove it from their eyes. These were not the eyes of young men. Hell, they weren't even the eyes of living men! My men were just boys, just like the Vietnamese boy I'd just killed. They'd been beaten down and fucked over and screwed with from the minute they set foot in this hellhole. But, for the most part, they didn't mind. These guys were not born rich. They were not the scions of important fathers. They were not destined for great things. The best of them, if they were lucky, would become cops or firefighters or shop foremen. They would never gain, make or be part of what the world deemed "history." But today, soaked to the bone, caked with mud, hoping for little more than a shower and some hot food, these kids were the sharp end of the spear in the mightiest army in the world. They walked a narrow tightrope between innocence and insanity, knowing, like me, they would never be who they used to be. They would never again be called young. They hoped and prayed their best years weren't behind them even as they dreaded what lay before them. They clung desperately to the sad, shitty shred their lives had become.

And I was their leader.

I walked them through the densest jungle in the world. I ran them against entrenched positions and into enemy fire. I flew with them into hot landing zones where bullets ripped through the skins of helicopters like buzz saws. I bandaged their wounds and listened to their sad stories about love lost. I told them my dumb-assed stories about all the ways I'd fucked up my life because the stories made them laugh even while they made me want to cry. I protected them and I defended them. I taught them and I did my damnedest to keep them out of harm's way. I berated them and I encouraged them and most of all, I loved them. I loved them more than any people on earth. I knew the machine gunner was right. I'd been alongside them through all the blood, death, and fire of this madness that was war. I hardly knew some of them but I loved all of them and now, frozen in this singular moment in time, I realized the immutable, unalterable truth. I was nothing without these kids. I could yell and scream and preach my own independence but I knew now that I was inextricably tied to them. They followed me and they trusted me. They were confident that even as I led them into danger I wouldn't waste their courage or their lives. I might not like it but I couldn't ever betray that trust by walking out on them. What difference did it make now if I wanted to save myself? I could stop being a soldier for myself but I could never stop being a leader for them. I might die here and I would certainly never psychically survive this but I had to keep going. I called them my squad but now I knew I belonged to them.

I turned in the direction I'd thrown my rifle.

"Doc, come with me and help me find my rifle."

The radioman already had it. They knew me too well.

"Here you go, Sarge."

Here we go indeed.

CHAPTER NINE

THOSE THAT I GUARD

"Those that I guard, I do not love.
Those that I fight, I do not hate."
•William Butler Yeats

The choppers whirled off in a swirl of dirt and debris, unloading the last of us. One hundred and seventeen guys knelt in the low grass and waited. Of course, it was me they were waiting for. My squad was on the point for our little foray into some uncharted jungle we were told was a way station for the bad guys.

I always wondered why, if the great strategists in the rear knew where the enemy was with such certainty, we didn't just bomb the piss out of an area and then send us in to see what survived. Somehow, the guys making decisions for peons like us always saw more value in risking the lives of a hundred guys than dropping a few hundred bombs.

My time to analyze the motives of the great thinkers was reduced by something more immediate. We'd only gone a few dozen meters into the trees when my point man signaled to me. I moved up and saw what was holding him up. It was smiling at me with a toothless grin that said we weren't alone in this part of the jungle. The firing port of a bunker loomed large just ahead of us. I signaled to the squad to hold in place while I went forward toward the bunker. If it was manned, I wouldn't have to worry about who was making decisions anymore. My luck held though and it was empty. I knelt in the dirt and picked up a handful. It was cool. It hadn't had time to be baked by the heat that was trapped under the jungle canopy. This thing was brand new. The VC must have been working on it when they heard our choppers. This was definitely not good. I looked back at my guys and noticed something on the backside of one of the tall palms that ringed the landing zone. There were lengths of bamboo hammered up the tree like rungs. They led to a small platform on the back of the palm.

Goddamn, I thought, we are already in deep shit.

I was contemplating my next move when the radioman slithered over to me.

"It's Six and he sounds pissed."

"He's always pissed," I said, kneeling down.

The radioman hesitated before handing me the handset.

"That man been hatin' on you since you got that bullshit medal in the 'Yard village, man," he said. "You best be cool with him."

I took the handset.

"Six, one-one, over."

The croak of the captain ground into my ear.

"What the hell is the hold up? We're all exposed in this LZ waiting for you to get moving!"

"Six, I'm taking it slow because we've got company out here. I've got a freshly dug bunker here and an observation post in one of the palms at the northeast edge of the LZ. We are definitely not alone here."

"One-One that's why we're here … to find these bastards and kill them... I'll send some one to check out the tree… now move out!"

The unwilling led by the unknowing, I thought as I handed the handset back to the radio guy.

"Keep that prick off my back, will you? Once an asshole, always an asshole."

"That man is sure enough trying to kill your white ass, Sarge," the radioman said.

I got up and started into the jungle.

But I ain't going to let him, I thought. Not now, not ever.

I made it another fifty meters and found a well-beaten trail running east and west. Barely camouflaged along the edge of the trail were two strands of communication wire. A bad situation was getting worse by the minute. The radioman moved forward and started uncovering the wire. There weren't two strands but eight.

"Kiss my ass," I whispered.

"Don't worry, Sarge," the radioman said softly. "Mr. Charles already be close enough to kiss your ass. We in some deep shit here."

"That's a roger, my friend. There are a whole lotta gooks who watched us land. They know how many guys and what kind of weapons we have. I just hope they don't have more guys than we have."

I took the handset and reported the latest finding to Six.

"Duffy, just pick a direction and follow the wire down the trail," was the response.

"Just pick your nose and follow it into your mouth," the radioman mumbled.

"That's a negative, Six," I said, trying to contain my rage. "These wires don't connect to a goddamned phone booth. We got a lot of gooks talking to each other on either flank of us right now.

"They were digging in when we landed. They've been watching us, counting us and our weapons. In a few minutes, we are going to be in the middle of a shit storm, Six. Pull us back. Call in the jets. Toast 'em--and then we can walk back in and count crispy critters... over."

"No jets, Duffy! No bombs! No napalm! We can handle this! You just pick a direction and move your butt out to follow the wire! That's an order!"

As the radio crackled with our voices but the air was full of our mutual hatred for each other. My squad assembled around the radio.

"Six... that's not an order! That's suicide! Pull us back around the LZ and bomb this motherfucker before a lot of us get dead."

"Duffy, if you don't have the guts to carry out my orders and engage the enemy, maybe you better get off the trail and let me send some real soldiers up to do the job."

My hands balled up into gnarled fists and the hate oozed out of me with my sweat.

Don't have the guts? I thought. I'll show him who's got guts. I was actually prepared to die to prove a point to an imbecile. And in that instant, I was as dumb as the dickhead giving the orders. Just about then I felt the stares of my men scorching into me – twelve sets of eyes all making the same plea. My guys were voting with their expressions. So this wasn't just about the captain and me. Even if I wanted to waste my life, I couldn't waste theirs. It wasn't about courage. It wasn't about honor. This was about pigheaded stupidity wearing the foppish disguise of courage. Now I knew what the old sarge told me about taking care of my men. I might be able to take the challenge myself, stupid as I might be. But I couldn't do it to them. They were still kids but they would never, ever be young again. They had hardly begun to live and yet they were perched on the edge of death. They wanted only to live and so many assholes stood in the way of that simple desire. I wasn't going to be one of them.

"Six, it looks like we've done as much as it can up here. If you have someone you think better equipped than us to handle this situation send 'em on up. Out."

"Get out of the way Duffy... I have some real troops heading to the point," the captain said.

The words were a drill bit in my ear.

Fuck it, I thought, it don't mean nothing. This ain't about him and me; it's about me and him and them.

I got the guys spread out to provide cover for the new point element.

When the new squad came forward, the point man looked like he'd just shit his pants.

"What have we got, Duffy?" the point man asked.

"An asshole for a captain," I said. "Be careful out there.

You got commo wire and a fucking three-lane gook highway. We are definitely not alone, amigo."

With those words in his ears, the point man crept onto the trail and followed the wire just as he'd been told. We watched the new point element disappear around the bend, with Six following. The captain sneered at me as he passed. I winked in response.

"I got you for disobeying a direct order, Duffy. This isn't over."

"It's not a good idea for the command element to be with the point, Six," I said, reminding him of infantry protocols. He scowled his usual scowl and went forward. Less than a hundred and twenty seconds later the point man was dead. The doc who jumped into the tiny clearing to help him was killed ten seconds later. On top of that, the Six lay bleeding and dying in the brutal sunlight of the clearing. All three had been riddled with steel fragments from a remote-detonated mine.

We hunkered down when we heard the first blast and the rapid volley of small arms fire that followed. I wanted so fucking hard to gloat that all the signs had pointed to this end but there wouldn't be time for anything now but fighting. This jungle was crawling with bad guys. I listened for more sounds coming from the ambush site and had my rifle aimed at the trail when a GI came running around the bend.

"Duffy... the point man got wasted and so did the medic... Six is fucked up real bad. The lieutenant wants your squad up there on the double!"

"Roger that!" I said, moving back to collect the men. "First squad! Saddle up. The Six stepped in shit!"

We charged around the bend into another unknown. A high berm rose along the left side of the trail. About fifty meters farther, I saw a cluster of GIs ringed around a gap in the berm. I went straight to the lieutenant.

"What do you need, sir?"

"Duffy, the captain's down and hurt bad. He'll die unless we can get him back here."

I scrambled to the top of the rise to see what we had to work with. It wasn't much. The three Americans lay prone in what looked like a dry creek bed. The point man was blown all to hell. He took a full blast from a claymore mine and it tore big chunks of flesh from all over his body. No one could survive wounds like that. The hedgerow hiding the gooks wasn't more than fifty meters from the creek bed. The gooks weren't visible but they didn't need to be. That's where they were--dug in and desperate. The last seconds of life for the point man played out in my mind. The commo wire led through the breach in the berm and the point man followed it as he'd been instructed. When he approached the enemy foxholes, they cut him down. When the medic saw the point man go down, his reflex was to help him and he ran blindly to his death. The Six just blundered into the clearing in time to catch the hell of a claymore.

These men didn't have to die. They didn't have to get hurt. If the captain had listened, the area would have been smoldering with napalm fires now and they would have been counting charred VC bodies. I scrambled back down the berm.

The lieutenant was working quickly but calmly, sending squads around the top of the berm. I liked that about him. He was a good leader. Though we never spoke about it, I wondered if he didn't feel the same eeriness I did about being under fire. He knew what had to be done and he wasn't afraid to let us do it our way.

"I've got the other squads up on the high ground to fire suppressing fire, Duffy. We can lay down a cover of smoke and try to hide your ass while you get captain. Does that work for you?"

"I'll let you know when I get back, LT." We shook hands.

"What else do you need, Sarge?"

"A big horseshoe up my ass would help, sir." I was only half-kidding.

I hoped the fear trilling in my brain like an alarm bell couldn't be heard by anyone else. It clanged and banged off both ears before settling over my skull along with something lying in my stomach like a broken bottle. My bones felt like water and my hands began a slight tremble.

This was going to be anything but easy but I couldn't let the guys see that.

"First squad, over here," I yelled and the men lined up.

"We got a good guy down in the clearing. He's about fifteen

feet from the rise and he's fucked up pretty good. We gotta get his ass outta there so we can medevac him in time to keep his wife from collecting on his GI insurance.

" Our guys on the rise are going to keep the gook heads down. Those guys over there are going to pop smoke all over the place. With a little luck, we'll be able to snatch the friendly and make it back without a problem."

I didn't want to tell them it was the captain we were about to retrieve. That might have turned their fear into rebellion, their 'why me?' into 'hell no!'

I took a rope from one of the men and hustled back to the gap in the berm. I was tying it to a grenade when the lieutenant approached.

"What's the rope for, Sarge?"

"With all the smoke and shit blowing around, I want to make sure I crawl to the right place, LT. The weight of the grenade will get the rope close to the captain's body then I can just follow the rope."

"Aren't you afraid the grenade might accidentally pop?"

"On the list of shit I'm afraid of right now, sir, the grenade is the last thing."

I swung the weight end of the rope a few times until I thought I had the right distance and let it fly. It plopped down within a yard or two of the wounded captain.

I turned to the radioman.

"We don't need a radio for this one. You stay here."

I couldn't tell if he looked relieved or disappointed.

"Stay low and close. When the shooting starts, we follow the rope out to wounded guy and drag him back. I'll take the body. The rest of you lay down covering fire.

"What's the rope for, Duffy?" the lieutenant asked.

"Right now, LT, I'm gonna use it to find my way to the GI. When I get back, I may use it to hang the motherfucker who sent good men out there to die."

I threw the rope as close to the captain as I could. My guys clustered around the gap, waiting for the call. Some of the men bounced from one foot to the other, like boxers shuffling around before a title fight. Others mumbled semi-silent prayers as the time grew nearer. I surveyed my flock.

"Stay close and stay low. When the shooting starts, we follow the rope out to the wounded guy and drag him back. I'll take the body. The rest of you guys lay down fire. Just rake that tree line. You don't need a target. We just need volume of fire. Stay low and keep your heads down and we'll all get out with our asses in one piece."

I looked into each man's eyes and gave them a smile. Now, if only I believed that.

"OK, LT, let that shit rip!"

The jungle jumped to life. The riot of the rifle and grenades numbed the senses and shattered the psyches of everyone near the clearing. Even guys shielded by the high berm got lower and started to cringe. Bullets cracked in the stagnant jungle air and whistled overhead. Our red tracers ripped into the trees and were answered by the VC green tracers. From the far side of the berm, the popping of smoke grenade pins prefaced the billowing clouds of red and purple and green smoke that clouded the clearing in a swirl of mingling colors.

"Here we go, boys!"

I led six men into the gap in a rushed, flailing low crawl that was all elbows and knees. The North Vietnamese knew what was happening and added their weapons to the chaos. The noise was denser than the smoke. It was mind-blowing, the din and clamor of men trying to kill each other.

The swirling colors provided cover but stung my nose. The crack of bullets overhead echoed in my ears but I crawled ahead, already in the "zone" where I felt calm, the stark fear all but forgotten as I focused on the mission to rescue the captain. My guys trailed behind me and popped single shots into the tree line but I felt totally detached from the action, more an observer than participant.

A machine gun opened up from the berm behind me and the rattle grew louder until it resonated and echoed in my chest. The exploding smoke grenades touched off small grass fires and the gray smoke intruded into the pallet of artificial smoke and grew even worse for my eyes. Puffs of dust kicked up where bullets struck the ground around me, the closer the puffs, the faster I crawled. The insane noise of the mad minute almost ruined my senses. It was easy to forget the virulent, angry heat; the stinking sweat of fear; the notion that each breath I breathed could be my last. In the eye of the storm, and through the chaos and confusion, I knew what needed to be done. Every hair on my body stood at attention. The threat of death made every nerve tingle. Every breath was intoxicating and made me euphoric knowing it could be my last. I was glad I was alone now, buried in the bowels of the battle, shielded by smoke and soot from the eyes of my men.

They would never see the narcotic effect of excitement that drove me in these moments of stark terror and head-splitting excitement. They would never know how much I feasted on being able to function when fear and chaos paralyzed other men. The smoke, the sweat, the noise, the confusion ... in the eye of the storm; it was a song to me and cacophony to the others.

I touched the captain's boot and felt blood dampen my hand. I inched forward until I was even with the wounded man's face. I turned the captain over to face him and found myself staring into the chiseled, bloody features of Bone Six. I grabbed him by the shirt and wiped some of the blood from his face, a face that looked like it had been carved out of stone. It was a sparse, feature-less face, almost skeletal, nothing but sharp angles and hard turns. He began to cough and a froth of pinkish foam issued from his mouth.

"You stupid fuck," I whispered in his ear, "they die and you live. It ain't right, you prick."

I grabbed a blade from my belt and snatched the captain roughly by the forehead. I jerked his head back, exposing a gaunt throat reddened with sunburn. The captain's eyes grew wide and gurgling sound caught in his throat. Pink froth spit from his voiceless mouth. I managed a smile while the wind of the war swirled over us.

"This won't hurt a bit, Six," I said, smiling.

I got the blade under the captain's jaw, near his throat. I popped an ugly black shrapnel fragment from his neck.

"There, captain," I said, showing him the fragment. "If your sorry ass lives, you can show your kids what their daddy did in the war."

Then I grabbed the captain's arms and again found my hands sloshing around in blood. He was tall and thin, all bones and knobs where most people have joints. I had little trouble moving him toward the gap as I jammed my heels into the jungle dust and pulled. Three pulls and I could hear the encouragement of the men behind the berm.

In front of me, I saw the smoke screen lifting. The deadly tree line was now a gauzy shape. Bullets spit out of the jungle in tongues of fire. My guys now vented their anger on the tree line and the crescendo rose. The Vietnamese could now see targets outlined and started firing on them. Incoming and outgoing fire battled evenly in a deadly competition. Neither side could see clearly but the lifting smoke was closing the window on what little safety we had. I felt the air split near my right ear as an angry shot whistled past. I gave another strained yank on the captain and felt the burden lift from my arms as a pair of GIs arrived and lifted the captain roughly to his feet. They half walked, half carried him back behind the safety of the berm. I saw the spreading dark blotches on the back of the captain's shirt and knew he must be in a world of hurt.

My ears throbbed from the noise and my lungs were about to burst from exhaustion. My nose was still full of the putrid stench of the smoke and cordite and burning grass. My face was streaked with a hideous mélange of purple and green and yellow smoke that made me look like something on a Mardi Gras float instead of a Vietnam battlefield. Otherwise, I was whole as I slid into the gap and around the berm wall. I fell back against the safety of the rise with an angry heart threatening to beat out of my chest as the scurry of jungle boots shuffled through the gap.

"Everyone back?" I shouted. "We still have everyone?"

The silence was more of an answer than words could have been.

"Who's down? Who's hit?"

The medic was bent over a prone figure, banging hard on the man's chest--twice, three times, one more time, savagely, and then he collapsed on the casualty.

"Who is it?" I asked.

"The new guy," the radioman said. "He caught one in the gut just about the time you made the snatch."

The medic bent over him and closed his eyes. I saw the peach-fuzzed face of a senior prom king.

"Motherfucker," I mumbled under my breath, "we just never stop paying for assholes like the Six."

The new guy was being covered by a poncho as I hurried by. A group of soldiers was frantically hacking at a stand of bamboo with machetes, bayonets, entrenching shovels and anything else remotely capable of chopping. Overhead, the whirring of the inbound evac chopper was audible over the confusion of the battle.

"Two minutes to touch down!" one of the radiomen yelled. "Let's get that bamboo cleared!"

I stood face to face with the lieutenant.

"What was the captain mumbling about, Duffy?"

"Beats me, LT I didn't have time to listen."

"He kept mumbling something about a bayonet."

"Shit, sir, you know how the wounded hallucinate."

"Well, you did a good job out there, sergeant."

I had started to walk back to the squad to tend to my dead soldier but stopped and turned to face the lieutenant.

"Good was never one of the choices, LT," I said. "Good is a memory. Here we choose between bad and worse. We never do anything good."

I walked away before I said something I'd regret. I wanted to say goodbye to a kid I never had a chance to know who would be making his last trip home.

'Where was the kid from?" I asked.

"Gum Creek, Mississippi," the radioman said.

"We never do anything good" I mumbled. "Never."

CHAPTER TEN

THE CASUALTY

I decided getting shot wasn't as bad as I thought. But that was only after the medic had hit me with a shot of morphine and swore on his mother's life I wasn't about to die. Whipping through the cold breeze in a medevac chopper at 3,500 feet with my nervous system on simmer, I thought I might be able to get used to this casualty stuff.

I wasn't nearly as enamored of it when the bullet had slammed into my ass and knocked me into the dirt of the Terre Rouge rubber plantation. I had an eight-man patrol walking through the rubber plantation on a routine reconnaissance mission when the shot rang out. By the time I heard it I was already lying in the red dirt with my ass on fire. I wanted to be mad and take some revenge on whoever had the balls to shoot me but every time I moved, a bullet kicked up near me. I lay still for a few moments to collect my thoughts and figure out what to do about this would-be assassin. I thought I'd better do something soon because I was feeling a bad combination of wooziness and nausea.

I saw a good-sized tree trunk not too far away and did the fastest low crawl I'd ever done to get behind it. The shots I'd seen – and felt – came from behind me and probably from above. So I started looking into the treetops for some sign of hostility. Nothing registered so I tried something else. The sniper was shooting only when I moved, so move I must. I started scrambling to another tree all the while searching the treetops. A volley came out of the trees and sprayed up some dirt way too close. I made it to the other tree and looked up while another bullet rained down.

There! I saw the rustling of the leaves. The sniper must have been pulling back his rifle and caught a branch. I switched to full automatic and fired a burst where I'd seen the branches move. Nothing happened so I fired another, and then another. The last one was the charm. An AK-47 came tumbling down from the tree. I never saw the guy and didn't know if I'd hit him but he didn't have a weapon any longer and that was good enough for me. When the rifle fell into the dirt, my squad started moving toward me. When they arrived I let them know how appreciative I was.

"Took you assholes long enough!" I growled. "I could

have been bleeding to death here."

The medic merely rolled me over and cut away my pants.

"I saw you get hit," the doc said. "I was concerned it was a brain injury."

"I get shot and everyone's a goddamned comic."

The doc was swabbing my butt cheek with something and then I felt the jab of the needle.

"Don't say I never gave you anything, Sarge. You won't even know you had an ass much less be ornery enough to act like one."

I couldn't think of anything amusing to say to a guy who just swabbed my ass so I just said thanks.

"Don't thank me, Duffy, I didn't do it for you. I did it for the poor nurses who are going to have to take care of you."

It didn't take long for the soothing heat of the morphine to start washing over me. I don't know how long it took for the medevac chopper to arrive but it wasn't long before the rarefied air washed over me and salved a bruised and blistered body that had more aches than it used to have places. The medic on the chopper told me of the delights that awaited me at the hospital.

"Great wound, pal," he said. "This will lay you up for a week to ten days. Hot chow, clean sheets, round-eyed nurses … don't get much better than that, GI."

It all sounded great to me.

My helicopter had company when we reached the hospital. Three more were landing as the stretcher-bearers were pulling me off the bird. They carried me into a big-ass tent where three giant fans were circulating the air. Three other teams of stretcher-bearers came in right behind me. The place went from busy to chaotic as more wounded were carried in. Our stretchers were placed on wooden sawhorses and the bearers headed back to the helicopter pad. They brought more wounded in.

Must be a shitty day in the war, I thought.

"Somebody will be out soon to take care of you, troop," one of the bearers said. Then he was gone and it was just the other wounded GIs and me. Calm replaced the chaos and only a few moans could be heard over the sound of the fans.

A few minutes later, a nurse in jungle fatigues came over, and I found myself looking into the prettiest eyes I'd ever seen – well, at least the prettiest I'd seen in Vietnam.

"Hey soldier, don't tell me you took this one charging," she giggled.

"Well, no… I was walking along…" She didn't let me finish.

"Hey soldier, it don't mean nothing. I was making a

little joke. You'll be fine. You won't be able to sit down for a while but ... hey ... butt ... get it?"

Very funny, I thought. I get shot and Goldie-fucking-Hawn is my nurse.

She wrapped a blood pressure cup around my arm and stuck a thermometer in my mouth.

"We're a little stacked up in the OR right now, Sarge, so we'll give you something for the pain and keep you out here where it's cool. We'll be along for you in a little bit, OK?"

I nodded knowing my response didn't much matter. I was going to be waiting my turn no matter what. The nurse held my wrist and in a few seconds she was gone. I was left to contemplate the whirring of the fan blades. I looked over my "roommates" on the other stretchers but no one made a sound. The nurse came back and rubbed something over the butt cheek without the bullet.

"This will sting a little but it will help you relax. This your first time, soldier?"

"Last time, lieutenant. Luke the Gook had his chance and he blew it. He's only going to get one chance."

"*Oh*, tough guy, huh?" she said, smiling. "They are in pretty bad shape but we'll be helping them soon. You just lie there and relax. We'll be along in a minute or two."

She hustled out of the room and the dope was taking

effect. I was feeling pretty good when I heard a low moan. It was the guy on the litter next to mine.

"Hey, guy, you doing OK?" I asked.

"C-c-c-c-c-o-o-o-o-l-l-l-l-d-d-d-d"

"You need my blanket, soldier?"

The only answer was another moan and some rustling on his litter. I stood on my shaky legs and with a spinning head I steadied myself against my stretcher until I got my bearings. The first step I took shot a bolt of pain up from my ass right into my brain but I made my way slowly over to the other stretcher with my blanket. I couldn't believe how small this kid looked. He's just a baby, I thought. His head was wrapped in a huge bandage that was probably white once but was now wet and red. A trickle of blood rolled out from under the turban and I automatically wiped it away before it found the wounded guy's eye. Even that faint touch made the kid wince.

"Sorry, kid, just trying to help."

The boy's face was a mess of burns and bruises and welts. Just about every inch of his face was puffed or bleeding or both. His eyes were little more than slits in badly swollen cheeks. I laid my blanket on him as gently as I could and looked at him for a long time. When another drop of blood seeped from the bandage, I wiped it away again. This time, the kid didn't move. Then I saw his mouth moving but couldn't make out what he was saying. I leaned in closer. The boy spoke with great effort.

"The straps hurt my arms," he said in a whisper.

I located the straps holding the kid on the stretcher and moved the blankets to find the buckles and loosen them. Then I understood why the boy looked so small. Both of his legs were gone, one at mid-thigh and the other just below the knee. Both stumps were wrapped in bloody bandages. I took a lot of care loosening the straps to ease the pressure on his arms.

A whisper ushered from the boy's lips and I bent down again to hear.

"Thanks, GI."

"My name is Duffy, soldier." I smiled to try to do something for him but he didn't respond. I took his hand when a litter on the other side of the room shook with violent spasms. I tried to move as quickly as I could with the pain coursing like electricity through my ass. I got to the other litter just in time for a jet of blood to splash onto my chest.

"Nurse! We've got a problem in here!"

I put my hand over the stream of blood jutting from his stomach and felt it bubbling through my fingers.

"Nurse! I need a hand in here!" I bet she would have thought that funny.

The blood wasn't stopping. It was running off the stretcher and splashing onto the concrete floor.

"Goddamn it, nurse! We need you in here!"

The nurse burst through the swinging doors and hurried to my side.

"Hey, tough guy, what are you doing out of bed?"

She moved my hand and slapped a thick gauze bandage over the wound. The pad was soaked in seconds. A spasm shook the body on the litter. The nurse took her hand off the wound and closed his eyes. Just like that, another soldier became a statistic.

Then she took my arm and helped me back to my stretcher.

"Where were you? I called but no one came. I didn't know what to do." I was surprised to feel tears welling up hot behind my eyes.

"It's OK. There isn't much that any of us can do. Some wounds are beyond our ability to fix. It's hard to understand how these guys survive at all."

"So you just let them die?"

"We don't *let* them do anything. We just can't save them all. That guy was ripped up inside by God only knows what. There was no way to stop all the bleeding. Now get up on the litter before you fall down. You've lost a good deal of blood and the Demerol is going to get your head spinning pretty soon."

I took her hand and let her help me onto my stomach. I looked over at the little kid next to me and my eyes must have asked what my lips couldn't.

She shook her head.

"He has massive head trauma, third degree burns and lots of internal bleeding. It's a miracle he didn't die out in the bush."

"Push me over there, will you?" I asked, nodding toward the kid next to me. She pushed me over and wiped off a lot of the blood from my chest and hands before checking on the boy's pulse.

"Behave yourself, tough guy," she reminded me, "you got shot, remember?"

"How can I forget?"

But I was talking to an empty room as she went through the doors.

I looked over at my new friend.

"How you doing, soldier?"

A hint of a smile was all he could muster in response. I got off the litter and stood beside him, wiping another blood drop from his face.

"You're doing great, kid. These guys will have you fixed up in no time."

The boy's mouth moved and I bent closer to hear him.

"I can't talk very good but I hear great," he said, "and I heard what she said."

Before he finished that sentence, I couldn't hold back the tears any longer.

"Fuck her, man. She don't know shit." I tried to smile.

"You fuck her," he whispered, "for me."

His burned and tortured lips turned up in the best he could do for a grin. That started me sobbing like a baby. This battered boy had endured so much in a life that gave him so little. He was just a bundle of suffering, his hope and usefulness expended, hanging onto life by the barest of threads and he was making jokes. I wanted to make someone pay for what they had done to this kid, what they had stolen from him, but who? The pain of my own wound was meaningless now, replaced by a pain so much worse, so much more persistent, and so much more permanent. I looked down at this broken body and wanted to scream my rage to the heavens. But heaven had long ago abandoned this hellhole.

"You hang in there, kid. What do you say we both do her?"

I bent low again to hear his response and heard a bad rattling sound in his chest.

"I'm going to pass," he said. "You do her twice."

My tears stung far worse than my bullet had. They fell off my face and on to the kid's bandages. I had to get out of there.

"How about I get us some water, kid?" I asked. "You thirsty? I'm parched."

The boy tugged at my sleeve.

"Please stay with me. Don't leave me. I don't want to die alone."

"No sweat, kid, I won't leave. I'm staying right here."

I could no longer see through my eyes. I was sobbing as I felt the kid's hand go limp in mine. Just like that he was gone, relieved of the pain that would now be another wound in my tortured psyche. I was still standing when the nurse returned.

"Hey, tough guy! "Get that ass, or what's left of it, back on the stretcher. We're ready for you now."

She saw me staring at the little kid's body.

"Poor kid. He looks so fragile and innocent, doesn't he?"

"Fragile, maybe," I said, "but you wouldn't believe what he wanted for his last request."

I woke up in the morning with my ass on fire from the network of stitches that seamed me shut. I'd prayed with all the old altar boy intensity I could muster to be delivered from this nightmare but the pain told me another prayer had gone unanswered. I was still wondering what I'd done to deserve this hell when the doctor came to my bed. He was holding a little metal object between his thumb and forefinger.

"Here's a little souvenir of your trip to Southeast Asia, sergeant," he said, dropping the bullet into my drinking cup. "Now that wasn't so bad, was it?"

He was talking about my wound but I was feeling something different.

"Doc, it was worse than anything you could imagine," I said.

It was worse than anything I could have imagined too, I thought.

CHAPTER ELEVEN

A MATTER OF DEFINITIONS

The ugly, gray-brown land leech inched its way up the dirty nylon of my boot. In a country so filled with shit to hate, I hated these slimy bastards more than anything. They looked like crawling snot. Even worse, they lived to suck the lifeblood out of anything they could attach themselves to. They were silent, relentless and insatiable, sinking their greedy little suckers into unsuspecting flesh without the decency to inflict pain. They sucked your blood without the dignity of giving any warning. One minute you were whole and the next these slimy bloodsuckers were feasting on your blood. Once upon a time, I heard it said that a sucking chest wound was nature's way of saying you were in a firefight. If that was true, leeches were nature's way of saying you were in hell. If Vietnam was the asshole of the world, leeches were its hemorrhoids.

I had no idea how these disgusting little fucks navigated but as an inducement, I pulled the pant leg up to expose the sickly white flesh of my leg. It had been five minutes since I noticed the slug slinking and slithering through its own slime to get up my boot. I waited until the shapeless blob fell on to my skin before taking it in my thumb and forefinger and squeezing it into a foul puree. A while ago, what seemed like an eternity ago, I would have been repulsed by the thought of killing any living thing. That was before I learned how to kill the enemy, the euphemism for saying I killed another man. Once you do that, killing a leech is no sweat.

Sarge had taught me the simple truth of combat a long time ago. It was just a matter of definitions. He told me to find a few friends I could depend on and learn to recognize the enemy. Keep the friends and kill the enemy, he said. It isn't any more complicated than that. Just that quickly, twenty years of morality and a few more of ethics dissolved into the single absolute of survival. Save the good. Kill the bad. I wiped the mess on my fingers into the filth already covering my pants.

One more enemy down, a couple million to go.

I ended my amusement with my latest kill and turned my attention back to the jungle. The triple canopy arched a hundred feet over the jungle floor. It was dark and solemn, like the church where I served Mass a couple life times ago. Streaks of sunlight crept through the trees and dappled the foliage below. That foliage was littered with tree trunks and fallen limbs, the losers in the fight to survive. Up in the treetops were the winners; the strongest that grew toward the sun and got the first of the rains. They had adapted and grown strong and tall. The rest had to compromise, to make do with what was left. The need to survive was everywhere. Even the jungle underscored the absolutes of Vietnam. It was hot and dry and then it was rainy. You suffocated in the heat or were soaked through during the monsoons. You were alive and breathing or you were sent home in an ugly rubber bag. It was pretty simple, really.

Scattered behind me were three FNGs. This was their first taste of life outside the barbed wire of the base camp. With any luck, the new guys would learn enough and know enough to become old guys. But that remained to be seen. At first they crouched and crept through the jungle like GI Joe, rifles ready and every muscle tensed but it didn't take long to recognize this observation post was the Vietnam equivalent of a walk in the park.

In front of me, the point man nestled in behind a thick tree trunk. He would be our early warning system should our peaceful morning turn ugly. The point man was every inch a soldier. I never saw anyone take to the Army so well or so seriously. It was as if he was born to do this stuff, which did not augur well for his health, mental or physical. I once called him the youngest lifer I'd ever seen. I thought it might get a rise out of him but all he did was smirk. So when the lieutenant tapped me for this routine mission, I still reached out to the point man. If there was someone I wanted with me in the event of an event, it was he.

I continued to scour the jungle for anything unusual, hoping to find only the usual. I turned my attention to the point man, watching him for any signs of trouble. He was sitting very still and then slid down behind the tree trunk.

This isn't good, I thought, as I lowered myself closer to the ground. I hoped that the three new guys might see me and do the same but they didn't. Where once they looked like they were going ashore at Normandy, they now talked and giggled like they were at Coney Island. I found a stone and threw it at the closest guy. He looked at me and got the message. All three pressed into the dirt.

That accomplished, I looked back to the point man. He had his shotgun pointed to the right so I started looking that way too. He loved that shotgun. Most guys on point carried an M-16. He liked the spray effect of the shotgun pellets, though. It had a real distinctive sound too so when he fired, I always knew where he was. I was hoping that whatever had spooked him was an animal of some sort but when I saw the flash of khaki, I knew we were in for some shit. I went into fight mode – controlling my breathing and trying to stay loose. I was taking shallow gulps of air and trying to counteract the surge of adrenalin that came at times like this. The VC was moving like I would have--slowly, cautiously, and carefully. I slid a grenade off my harness and started straightening the pin. I prayed silently that this guy was alone. We were not in great shape to be engaging any kind of force with just five guys.

The VC was now only ten meters away but in the thick jungle, it might as well have been a mile. I could see only the color of his uniform and he had no idea we were stalking him. I slid the pin out of my grenade and looked for a place to throw it. Before I could decide, I heard the shotgun blast up ahead. I rolled the grenade across the jungle floor as far away from me as I could and switched my M-16 to automatic. I blasted ten rounds at the khaki form and watched it fall. Two more blasts from the shotgun turned my attention toward the point man, and I made it forward in a low crouch but the point man didn't need me. Two were down, one dead and the other dying while clutching a handful of guts and spitting blood. The rest of his life was counting down in seconds.

I motioned to the new guys to check the other VC and they crawled toward him cautiously. I walked back before they made it there. The poor bastard was a mess. He took a bullet to the shoulder and another to the chest. But the grenade had done the real damage. His leg dangled by a shard of skin. The meat of his calf had been gouged out by the blast and only adrenalin was keeping him alive.

There was a time when I might have been frantic in my efforts to try to save this guy. Now, though, I knew I was possessed with an infinite capacity to kill but painfully limited skill to heal. I knew neither guy was alive in any real sense and they were suffering beyond my ability to comprehend. I put a round into the man's head and ended his pain. A few meters away, a shotgun blast echoed and I assume the point man had done the same for his guy.

I used the radio to report the action and got orders to wait for Six to arrive and check things out.

"You three–set up security up front," I said. "The captain is coming out for a look-see."

I took a tropical chocolate bar from my pants. I moved away from the body as thousands of flies homed in on the mangled corpse. After a few tries, I managed to break a piece of the chocolate off and stuffed it in my mouth. Over the sound of my teeth crunching the chocolate, I heard a voice way too loud for the jungle.

"I don't care if he hears me! I want him to hear me!"

Who the… I wondered.

The point man walked over to the new guy with the big mouth.

"Where the fuck do you think you are, asshole? Keep your fucking voice down," he warned, as the other two new guys shrunk back. "What the fuck is your problem, shithead?"

The loud FNG stood his ground.

"You! You and the Sarge are the problems! You two murdered two wounded soldiers and I'm reporting you for it!" The sound of his voice might as well have been a bass drum resonating through the jungle.

I needed to put and end to this bullshit quickly. I was walking over to the new guy when I heard the words "murderer" and "sarge." That made me move a little quicker.

"You pussy motherfucker!" I said, giving him a straight arm and knocking him on his ass. "I should break your fucking neck."

"Go ahead, asshole. Kill me the way you killed those other two men!"

I was getting more pissed off with every sound the FNG made. I grabbed the new guy by the throat and then felt a firm hand on my shoulder.

"Easy, Sarge. Don't let the asshole get to you," the point man said.

I let asshole go and let him regain his feet. I prayed he'd take a swing at me.

"You murdered those men in cold blood," the new guy said. "They were helpless and wounded and you killed them. That's murder and you will pay for it."

"That's war, you fucking moron. They were dying and suffering and they were better off dead. Maybe if you'd spent more than ten minutes in the bush you'd understand that, you fucking newbie!"

I was fully prepared to let it go at that but the sneer of contempt on the new guy's face pushed me over the edge.

He hasn't been here long enough to hate anything, much less me, I thought.

I lunged at the new guy and grabbed him by the back of the shirt. I half walked him and half dragged him over to the body I'd killed. I threw him onto the blood-soaked ground next to the corpse. I mashed his face into the bloody mud for a few seconds. I pulled him to his feet.

"How does that feel?" I asked. "You like the smell of blood? You like the stink of death? You might get to like it, just because it ain't yours.

"That's the stink of someone who would have gladly killed your green ass if it wasn't for me and the guy over there. You think you're some kind of judge about what goes on out here in the bush? You wait a few days and see how you judge things. In the meantime, know you're sorry ass is alive because of me and the point man."

"Fuck you, sergeant. I don't need either of you to protect me. You're a murderer and you're going to pay for that."

I let that slide. This guy meant nothing to me now. I could see the concern on the point man's face though.

"What's up?" I asked.

"If these fucking newbies report us, Sarge, we could be in big trouble."

"For what? We did the right thing, man. Don't be second-guessing yourself."

"How many times have you told me we never get to do the right thing, Sarge? You always told me we chose between bad and worse. So what did we do today, bad or worse?"

I was dumbfounded. I hated this place, this killing, this suffering – all of it more than anyone and now I'm being called a murderer? This is insane, I thought, but then remembered this whole fucking place was insane.

The point man continued.

"I know none of this means shit to you, Sarge. This time next year, you'll be back in college and studying Shakespeare or one of those fancy talking dudes but this is my life, man. The Army is my new home. That's why I'm here, to make quick rank, more pay and all that. These new guys are fucking with my life."

What kind of bullshit is this? I wondered. Here's a good, honest, decent guy who wants nothing more than to be a soldier and newbie is threatening all that. Sarge always told me to keep the friends and kill the enemy. It wasn't any more complicated than that. Keep your friends and get rid of your enemies. I think I can do that.

I put my hand on the point man's shoulder.

"Don't worry. I'll take care of this."

The point man looked at me and sensed what I was about to do.

"Don't do anything stupid, Sarge," he said.

"Stupid is over there, man" I said, pointing to the new guy. "What I am going to do won't be stupid."

I was still staring at the new guy, plotting my strategy when I saw a bright red spray blossom from the new guy's head. He stayed upright for a second or two and then folded up like a puppet with his strings cut. We all hit the dirt.

"Sniper!" I yelled, warning the detail coming from the LZ of the new danger. "This guy can shoot!"

Another of the new guys was spooked and got up to run. The point man went after him and tackled him just before a shot hit the tree in front of them.

"Stay down and live, asshole," he said.

The radioman coming up with the CO called in some mortar fire on the jungle and we didn't hear anything more from the sniper. The platoon was spreading out in the jungle and we got a break from the action.

"Hey, Sarge, you weren't really going to off that kid, were you?" the point man asked.

"It ain't complicated, man," I said. "We've got a mission and when someone threatens the mission, you never know what'll happen. Let them send this guy back to the World as a hero in the great struggle against godless communism."

I smiled a little to think I'd just about given up on God.

CHAPTER TWELVE

OLD TIMES THERE ARE NOT FORGOTTEN

The down times in Vietnam are two-edged swords. The good side means you aren't exposing your young ass to too much danger. Even in the rear, a stray mortar or rocket might hit you but I'd take those odds any day over humping the jungle. The other side was having way too much time to think and thinking wasn't always good. I spent too much time knee-deep in the past, dwelling on the catastrophic failures that landed me in this place. I thought too much also about what might lie ahead. As a grunt in Vietnam, I knew nothing good was waiting for me down the road so I just stewed in the past. But down times never lasted. There was always somebody to kill. When I was summoned to the battalion commander's tent at oh-dark-thirty, I knew I wasn't about to receive any good news. And I didn't.

The old man was droning on about duty and courage and kicking ass and a lot of other nonsense that served only to fill the tent with noise. I stopped listening after the colonel gave me the news that my squad was to lead a hill assault in a couple of hours. That started the familiar and awful crawl of fear in my stomach. I started to tingle, like my blood had begun to percolate. Sweat started its course down my back and into my pants. No matter how many times I'd endured shit like this I could never shake the feeling that this mission could be the last–especially this mission. We'd fucked around on this hill twice in recent months. Each time, we'd taken casualties and each time we abandoned the place as soon as we took it. Each time also, the bad guys came back to occupy the high ground from which they could observe and attack. It had been two months but it seemed like yesterday that we'd assaulted up the reverse slope of this hill. Three guys bought it that day and I was still carrying shrapnel from one of a hundred grenades they rolled down at us.

I caught some "honor" phrases and a couple of "courage" metaphors and a lot of other bullshit before the colonel mercifully ended his rant with a prayer that our God above would smile on us trying to blow the shit out of the other guys. I was pretty sure the bad guys would offer similar prayers to Buddha so all that remained was to see whose God had spare time that day. I thought my bookie back in the World would have lined this contest Buddha minus three. The backdrop to my musings was the rumbling of artillery that had been blasting the hilltop since the lieutenant and I had been called to the tent. The bombardment would help a little but I was still faced with the certainty that some of my guys were going to get it on this goddamned hill–again. I started planning my strategy on the walk back to the squad. I interrupted it to question the lieutenant.

"The old man knows there are other squads in this fucking company, right?"

"He knows, Duffy, but he also knows who he can count on."

"Oh God, LT, spare me that bullshit. Counting on me isn't going to help my guys who get hit going up this fucker. Why don't we just put an escalator on the hill since we go up and come down so much."

"Just do your job, Duffy," the lieutenant said, trying very much to sound like an officer. But then he added:

"Good luck."

Luck my ass, I thought. Luck isn't going to mean much since Luke the Gook has been through our assaults before and knows what to expect. I got back to the squad and avoided looking them in the eyes. I knew what I'd see. Some of them were trying to put on a tough façade. Others looked scared as hell. A couple had tears dangerously close to leaking out. No one wanted to look as scared as they were. I needed to make them stop thinking about fear and get them thinking about what they had to do.

"First squad, saddle up! We're moving out! Step fucking lively, boys. We got us another adventure!"

The guys hitched up their gear and checked magazines and machine gun ammo. I yelled over to the machine gunner.

"Grab another can of ammo! We're going to use bullets instead of bodies to take this mother this time."

I walked among the guys giving them encouragement and trying to get their heads in the game. You dwelled on fear and sooner or later that shit caught up with you. I wanted it to be later, much later. I turned to the radioman.

"Make sure Apache Six knows where we are all the time. I don't want any friendly fire raining down on us, you dig?"

"Gotcha, Sarge. I be taking good care of yo' ass today. You do the same for me, 'K?"

"It's a deal," I said as we headed off toward the birds that would carry us to the foot of the hill.

I was getting my guys settled when the colonel approached. He surprised me. The brass rarely got this close to us at the start of a mission. He walked up to me and put his hand on my shoulder.

"Sergeant, your men are the best we've got. Show those gooks what GIs are made of. And when you win the crest, fly this flag proudly, son."

He stuffed something in my pack and was gone.

Asshole, I thought. No one will win anything today. If I stay alive I'll be happy. I jumped on the chopper and we were off.

Fifteen minutes later, we landed in the usual storm of dust and twigs and sticks. Fifteen seconds later, the choppers were gone.

I got the guys together and laid out the plan.

"We ain't charging willy-nilly up this fucking hill any more," I said. "I want the machine gun team to move over to the right flank. Go about a hundred, a hundred and fifty meters out there. Move up a couple hundred meters and start hammering the hilltop with bullets. Then move up a little more and repeat. Save some ammo for the last dash.

"Grenadiers, I want you to do the same over on the left flank. Get up the slope and find some cover. Then keep firing for a couple minutes and move up some more.

"I'm going to take Bravo team right up the middle

and hopefully keep these bastards focused on us. We can confuse them a little if they start taking fire from each flank. We OK? Let's get it done."

I spread my four guys out and started up. The teams were moving quickly on the flanks and I wondered how far up we'd get before they opened up on us.

The radioman was behind me and yelled up:

"Switching to aerial rockets!" The aerial rocket artillery (ARA) started ripping great gouges in the trees and the earth. Some of the gunships blasted their rockets. Other gunships used their mini-guns to rake the hilltop. The whoosh and boom of the rockets and woodpecker sound of the mini-guns was like music to us grunts and I prayed they would soften things at the summit a little.

"Get on the gunship freq and tell them where we are. I don't want my own men to kill me today!"

The rest of the company was arrayed behind us, inching up as we made progress on the point. Other platoons had their point elements going up other locations on the hill.

The slope got steeper and the climb got harder. I was sweating rivers under my steel pot and the water kept running into my eyes. I kept moving, as I knew there wasn't going to be much to see for another hundred meters. I had a running total clicking in my mind as we passed every meter.

Christ, could it be this easy? I thought. No resistance

yet.

Then the machine gunner opened up a salvo from the right and I saw the limbs snapping from trees.

"Let's go!" I yelled. "We've got their heads down!"

With the deafening roar of battle echoing around us, we double timed up the hill for another thirty or so meters. I held us up behind the cover of some fallen trees. Then the grenades from the grenade launchers went out. Clouds of dirt and debris followed the dull thump they made leaving the barrels when they landed with the whacking sound they made. The rocket runs of the gunships were over but they still made passes with their six-barreled mini guns ripping across the summit. The grenade launcher was more effective than they might have been since the near-continuous fighting on the hill had denuded it of foliage. The rounds were coming out on a flat trajectory and impacting around the summit. Then I heard the machine gun open up again from the right.

"Up we go, guys!" I yelled as I crept over the tree trunk. We moved quickly, in a low crouch and covered a decent amount of ground. I dropped us behind some big rocks just fifty meters below the crest of the hill.

"Put covering fire on the hilltop so the flanks can move up!" I screamed and we all started putting M-16 fire on to the crest. With all the guns blazing, I took a chance and started up. I heard the reassuring chatter of the machine gun from the left and the gun was already higher on the hill than I.

We might just make this motherfucker, I thought as I sprinted from one shattered tree trunk to another. A grenade came rolling down the hill and I dropped low in the dust. The explosion covered me in dirt but left me unharmed so I started up again.

I didn't see the second grenade. It must have come over my head and exploded behind me, catching my back with shrapnel. The impact knocked me forward and I felt the burn of the hot metal in me. I rolled over on my back to see if I could rub some of it out but rolled back on my stomach and dealt with the pain as well as I could. I was only twenty or so meters from the crest, so I struck out again.

I made it a few meters before a bullet slammed into my side like a scalding sledgehammer. It knocked me backwards, down the slope and against a broken tree trunk. But the impact and the fall made me lose my rifle. I was hurt and helpless and vulnerable as hell. My side was on fire but I tried to feel around and find my rifle when I heard the scream. I looked up to see a bad guy running down the hill toward me.

Goddamn, I thought, I'm going out without even getting a chance to fight back.

I heard the gunshot and waited for the end. But I didn't end. The VC was knocked backwards and twenty or so machine gun rounds made his body jump like he was being electrocuted.

"I think you got him," I said to the machine gunner. "Save some rounds for the summit."

"Shit, Sarge, we already took the summit," he grinned. "While you were fucking around over here, we went right up the flank and got into their holes. Next thing I knew, we were all alone. The gooks must have di-di-ed."

Di-di-ed again, I thought. They were never going to stay and fight. They left one unlucky fuck behind to slow things down so they could get away.

The medic appeared again like magic.

"Sarge, you are one lucky SOB," he said as he slapped a patch over my side and another one on my back. "The round was a through and through. Passed right through your side and left you with two nice little holes."

"Lucky, my ass, doc. Lucky is when they miss."

"Can you stand," the doc asked. "It will be easier to get a bird in here if we get to the top."

I stood and was surprised at how little it hurt. I felt a sting from both holes but the shrapnel in my back hurt worse. But I could walk so I could make it to the top. We found a few bodies that had probably been killed by the choppers. One bad guy had definitely been hit by a mini-gun blast. The mini-guns fired at such a rapid rate it was said one could put a machine gun bullet down on every three inches of a football field. This poor bastard was evidence. The first round hit him in the ankle and stitched holes all the way to his head. Or maybe it happened the other way around. At any rate, he had bullet holes all up the right side of his body. The rest of the company was making its way up the hill as I surveyed the damage. We must have spent a million dollars of ordnance to kill four or five guys and take a shitty hill we called 729. What a fucking waste …

My ears perked up when I heard the radio guy talking to the colonel's helicopter.

"That's affirmative. Apache one-one is on the summit."

What the fuck did it matter to the CO if I was at the top? I wondered. For all he knows, I got wasted.

"Six wants to know where the flag is?" the radioman said.

"Oh shit, I forgot all about his goddamned flag, what with getting shot and all. What an asshole.

"Come here and get it out of my pack."

The radioman reached behind me and pulled out a flag. But it wasn't the stars and stripes.

The radioman held it up and said:

"Well ain't this some shit?"

He was holding the state flag of Georgia, a flag that prominently displayed the stars and bars of the Confederacy for all my black soldiers to see. My pain was nothing compared to the anger I was feeling.

"Throw that thing in the fire over there. Tell the colonel I lost it on the way up."

The radioman smiled and mumbled into the handset.

But that didn't stop the colonel. Five minutes later, his bird landed in a blinding cloud of ash and dust. He jumped off all starched and spiffy looking. It didn't take long for him to find a suitable tree trunk on which to fasten the Georgia flag. To no one's great surprise, a photographer got off the chopper and snapped off a series of pictures.

"The old man taking his fuckin' yearbook picture," the radioman said. "But he sportin' a nigger-hatin' flag 'stead of a football."

Pictures all taken, the Six went over and shook hands with our captain and then with the lieutenant.

The radioman and some of the other black soldiers started singing in low, but audible, tones.

> *"I wish I was in the land of cotton.*
> *Old times there are not forgotten.*
> *Look away, look away, look away …*
> *"Dixieland."*

"Duffy, you need a ride to the aid station?" the captain asked. "You're hit? The colonel says you can ride in his bird."

"I'm OK, sir. If it's all the same with you, I'll wait for the next one."

The helicopter whipped off the blasted hilltop in another rain of soot and dirt. I went over to the flag and ripped it off the tree. I tossed it into the spider hole where the VC had died.

"Old times there are not forgotten," I sang.

CHAPTER THIRTEEN

WAR WITHOUT GLORY

Looking back through the haze of misty memories, I'm not sure if she was as beautiful as I recall or if that part of the experience was a creation of my imagination. But it didn't really matter. She smelled of soap. That was enough to make me fall in love. She had round eyes that were an exotic green. She spoke English without the pigeon accent. She smiled with bright white teeth and she had the softest hands that ever touched me. In a word, she was a nurse and she made that trip to the hospital something worth remembering.

I was evacuated from the battle for the hill on a medevac chopper and brought to this hospital. I encountered none of the drama had marked my previous visit. There were only a few guys waiting with me and they weren't emergency cases. Mine was the worse wound so I got ushered in quickly where the doc hit me with a needle and a probe that went all the way through the wound in my side.

"You are a lucky guy," the doc said.

"No, lucky is when they miss, doc," I answered. "What's the deal here?"

"The bullet went through your side, missed the ribs and all the vital organs in your mid-section. We'll pump some antibiotics into you to combat infection and you'll be back in the saddle in no time."

That definitcly isn't lucky, I thought. I had hoped this one might be the one that got me out of this hellhole.

They took me to a bed in a big long line of beds and that's where I first encountered Missy.

"My name is Melissa," she told me, as she wrapped my arm with the blood pressure cuff, "but everyone calls me Missy."

"Well, to me, you are LT Merritt," I said. "You out rank me."

"Call me Missy. You wouldn't want me to ignore you because you called me lieutenant."

So Missy it was. I only saw her when it was time for meds or pain shots. I actually started looking forward to the pain because it meant I would see her again. The other nurses were a blur. When Missy went off duty the loneliness that was always on the fringe of my mind elbowed its way to the forefront. When she came back in the morning, my mood swung back to the plus side. It wasn't because of her looks that I gravitated to her. The jungle fatigues the nurses all wore pretty much hid all the parts that might stimulate lust. They could have been there but you couldn't see them. It was more her manner, the way she smiled all the time and made everyone feel special because of the way she treated us. The fighting must have slacked off because there weren't many of us on the ward. One afternoon, after my pain shot, she sat next to my bed.

"How is it out there?" she asked. "Out in the field, I mean."

I was letting the luxuriating wave of euphoria from the Demerol sweep over me as I relaxed to the sound of her voice. The question jarred me out of my high.

"It's fucking crazy out there," I blurted out. "Sorry, ma'am, I didn't mean to use that word."

"It's OK, soldier. It's not the first time I've heard it."

I made a mental note that I needed to learn how to talk to women again.

"Why did you say 'crazy'? Others have called it terrifying, horrible, disgusting and on an on. But no one ever called it crazy."

"It is utterly insane," I said. "We have no strategy

except killing. Body count is all anyone cares about. So we wander around in the jungle, sweating our asses off, hoping we won't have to add to the count."

She must have sensed I was getting pissed off so she stuck a thermometer in my mouth. It gave me time to think. That's wasn't good. If she thought I would calm down, she was wrong.

"We've got these young kids right out of high school," I went on. "Before they got here, the biggest decision they ever made was who to take to the senior prom. Now we teach them how to pick out targets to kill in our ambushes."

She got me wound up and now I was pretty sure she was getting more information than she needed but I couldn't stop.

"We teach them how to blow people in half with claymore mines. We teach them how to bandage each other up so their buddies don't bleed out when we're the targets. A couple weeks ago, an 18 year-old kid saved his buddy by sticking his hand into a big hole in the guy's leg and pinching off an arterial bleed. What in your life prepares you for that kind of shit?"

Missy looked as though she was struggling to find an answer to my question.

"These kids will never be the same after this," I went on. "I see them evolve, or is it devolve, after a few firefights.

Their eyes give them away. They aren't kids anymore and they aren't yet men. They're something in between. Sometimes, you get kids who put their heads down and cry when the shit hits the fan. Sometimes you get a guy so gung-ho he wants to charge into the teeth of enemy fire.

"Then, after they go through all this lunatic shit, they will get a letter from home telling a guy his girl is screwing someone else. I actually had a kid ask me for a compassionate reassignment because his parents were getting a divorce. I tell him to clean his weapon and check his ammo and don't worry about all that shit at home."

Her eyes were glazing over and I thought I was boring her – until I saw the tears leak from her eyes. That didn't stop my rant.

"While I'm trying to deal with all their shit, I'm going through my own breakdown. One day, I shoot a guy in the mouth for throwing a grenade at me. The next day I'm all fucked up because I killed a kid who was shooting at me.

"If all that isn't crazy, I don't know what crazy might be. No one tells us anything. No one gives us reasons. No one can tell us if we're winning or not. No one gives a flying fuck about grunts. Sorry for the language, ma'am."

She looked at me after my rant and I saw her eyes misting up.

"God, Duffy, what are we doing here and when will it

all end?"

"I haven't got a clue, Missy, but I know that we are fucking up a bunch of people physically for sure but mentally just as sure," I said. "But in the meantime, you guys back here in the rear have it dicked: sleeping on clean sheets every night, hot chow every day, playing doctor with the docs …"

Before I could go on, she rose up. Standing over me, her face flushed with anger.

"You asshole," she said. "Dicked? Yeah, right. We've got it made in the shade here."

Right off, I knew I fucked up.

"All we do every day is deal with broken bodies. We see guys like you come in here all day and night," she said, her voice rising. "They have wounds we've never seen much less treated with before. You are moaning about a kid pinching off an artery. How many times do you think we do that? Ever see burn victims? Ever see what napalm does to skin? Ever have to try to put a burned kid in a whirlpool to debride his wounds? Did you ever have to listen to the screams from those kids? "

She was really hot now. She started stripping pillows of their cases and put them back on the same pillow. She clanged a few bedpans into nightstands. She started to walk away but did an about-face and came back fuming.

"How many times do you think we deal with sad, dying kids crying for their mothers when pain they couldn't even conceive of wracked their broken bodies?

"How many times do you think we have to watch the light go out in those kids' eyes and feel utterly defeated because we couldn't save them?"

I tried to interject with an apology but I was too slow.

"You insufferable asshole!" she said. "What do you think happens after your little stay here? Do you think you are the only grunt in Vietnam who gets wounded? Do you know how many patients we see week after week, month after month? Do you know what it feels like to patch these kids up and send them back into that meat grinder? You think you know what goes on here?"

I thought that might warrant an answer that would convey my sorrow at having suggested the nurses had it made. But Missy was on a roll and she would not be stopped.

"Did you ever see the surgeons and their nurses after eight or ten hours in an operating room? You talk about the eyes of your kids. That's nothing compared to the eyes of the operating room staff dealing with a never-ending stream of battered patients.

"Other than that, we just sit around in our air conditioned luxury and wait for you to come back to us."

Her voice turned into a whisper.

"God, what a mistake I made with you. I actually thought you were different, Duffy."

She walked away, leaving me wounded again. Her words were as painful as any bullet. I wanted to be different. I wanted her to know that I was different but now I'm lumped in with all the assholes that come in and trying to cop a feel or thinking they could actually get laid. I was just another asshole, probably the worst kind because I insulted her and was oblivious to her war. I wanted her to like me and I ended up making her hate me.

I deliberately skipped my next pain shot, thinking the pain would be my penance for being such a douche bag. It didn't help.

I was an hour past due for my shot when she reappeared. She was still pissed.

"You want this or not?" she asked, holding up the needle.

"What I want is to say I'm sorry," I said. "I run my mouth way before my brain gets engaged. It comes from dealing with the assholes in the field. The answers to all your questions is no. I didn't consider the kind of shit you deal with every day. I was being a self-centered jerk and I'm sorry."

"Roll over," she said, injecting me with the joy juice.

"You're forgiven and I probably should apologize for going off on you."

"Hell no! Don't apologize for opening my eyes, for making me see what kind of war you fight every day. We all tend to think we have the shittiest job in the world. We think of anyone in the rear as a REMF – rear echelon motherfuckers. I never realized what you do when I'm gone. And that's my mistake, one I'll not make again."

I saw her eyes soften.

"Missy, you fight a strange and important war. Your weapon is the caring and compassion that you show all of us grunts. Your war is one without glory, not that there's a whole lot of glory in the bush. I'm an asshole for not appreciating what you all do here everyday."

"Yes, you are," she said, smiling. She touched my forehead and I'll never forget those hands. "Get some sleep, asshole. We'll have to send you back out in a few days."

All I heard was "asshole" as the warm bliss carried me away on gentle wings. She could call me an asshole any time.

A couple of days passed and I knew my time in the hospital was getting short. My wound stopped draining and all I could feel was the pull of the stitches when I turned or twisted. Missy had forgiven me. She showed that by sending a shrink to my bed. I went through all the mood swings

I'd been feeling and he pronounced me sane. He said I'd be insane if I wasn't feeling these swings. He did tell me, however, that I was exhibiting a man/superman complex.

"This is the true joy in life, being used for a purpose recognized by yourself as a mighty one; being thoroughly worn out before you are thrown on the scrap heap; being a force of Nature instead of a feverish selfish little clod of ailments and grievances complaining that the world will not devote itself to making you happy," he said, adding "this is a good thing." I thought the guy a genius coming up with that diagnosis and that assessment of my character. It wasn't until years later that I found out that the little shit was quoting George Bernard Shaw without attribution.

After the psychiatrist left, she came by my bed.

"Well, Duffy, I bought you a couple more days here. I put a note on your chart that said you spiked a fever last night and the doctor said to keep you a couple more days to check for infection."

I wanted to say something that would really demonstrate my appreciation, something witty and profound. All I came up with was "thanks."

Those two days went by all too quickly but, truth be told, I was kind of itchy to get back to the guys. I wondered how many times they'd managed to screw things up while I was gone. When I saw the REMF with the clipboard come through the ward, I knew my vacation was over. Guys with clipboards are always bad news.

"Duffy, Joshua, sergeant E-5!" he yelled.

"Hey keep it down, asshole," I responded. "There are wounded GIs in here. I'm Duffy. Let's go."

"Still being Superman," Missy said, winking at me. "Stay away from the kryptonite out there and go home in one piece."

"Thanks for everything, ma'am. When I get back to my unit, I'm going to tell everyone that nurses are an easy lay."

She swatted the back of my head and said:

"If you do, I'll come out there and find you and kick your ass."

I loved that girl.

CHAPTER FOURTEEN

THE EASY DAY

Later on, I would find out that we were placed astride something called the Serges Jungle Highway. It was a main route for the North Vietnamese and the Viet Cong to leave safe havens in Cambodia to attack Saigon. At the time, however, all I knew was we were in the jungle and we were fighting much more than usual. This Area of Operation didn't look like a highway by any means but the VC must have thought it one as the bad guys came pouring out of Cambodia almost daily. And they weren't at all happy that we kept killing them. So I was real surprised when my lieutenant said I was wanted back at base camp. When I arrived and reported to the battalion commander I thought I got some good news.

"We've named you 'soldier of the month' so you get

to take it easy for a couple of days, sergeant," the colonel said. "You've had a tough couple months."

"We all have, sir. This AO is a bitch."

"But we're doing a good job of keeping the NVA away from Saigon. That's our goal and our mission."

My mission was to stay alive long enough to get my ass out of Vietnam and the army, I thought. But I didn't tell the commanding officer that.

"Yes, sir. Mission first!" I said enthusiastically.

"Well enjoy your rest, sergeant. We're going to need you in good shape when we send you back to the field."

I smiled but said nothing. No matter what kind of shape I was in, the bush would wear me down to a nub--not just me, all of us. No one would come out of the way we lived and died out there and still be the same. I prayed I'd have enough of myself left to start living for real again. This creation the army made of me was not someone I wanted to be.

My stitches were gone and the wounds scabbed over. I was a little tight where the bullet had passed but I was feeling pretty good, all in all. I started running to get some of my endurance back and did hundreds of push-ups to go with daily runs. I was amazed and not in a good way at how much my time in the hospital had taken from the rugged warrior the army had made me. I was thinking how good it was of the CO to give me a chance to get back some of my strength when the first sergeant came out to see me doing calisthenics. The first sergeant was a good guy for a lifer but he was a stone drunk. Guys who would be in the rear for a while would always come back out with outrageous stories about the shit the first shirt pulled virtually every night. I thought that if I had no other options but to stay in the army for twenty years I'd be an alcoholic too.

"Hey Duffy, I got a little job for you to do," he called.

I stopped my push-ups and walked over to him.

"Yeah, what kind of job, Top?"

"I need you to take a little walk around the perimeter here and check things out."

"What kind of things?"

"Whatever the fuck you see that needs reporting, sergeant," he said in a growl. "I got some new guys who need the experience. Alpha Company blew an ambush on some gooks last night. They didn't get any bodies but there was a lot of blood out there. So keep your fucking eyes open!"

This was the army's version of take it easy.

"OK, Top," I said. "No need to get hostile. I was just asking."

"Well, report to company HQ in twenty minutes and we'll get this show one the road."

"You got it. See you in twenty."

This was exactly the kind of shit that happened when you were in the rear. If I weren't a non-commissioned officer, they would have had me burning shit or running garbage or some other nonsense that the REMFs could do. But as an NCO, I got the "good" assignment of doing a sweep around the perimeter with a bunch of FNGs. This was my "reward." But what the hell, I'll get hot food tonight and sleep on something that resembles a mattress. So off I went.

I got over to the company hooch with a few minutes to spare. I looked over my charges. They were greener than the shiny green of their fatigues.

"How long you guys been in country?" I asked.

"Almost a week," one of them answered. "I mean almost a week, sergeant."

I got a chuckle out of that.

"No need to call me sergeant. My name is Duffy and I'm your leader for today. Just do what I tell you when I tell you and we'll all be OK."

I had to evaluate these guys quickly.

"Where did you all do infantry AIT?"

They all started to yell out at once.

"Hold it!" I yelled. "One at a time… you first."

"Ft. Benning, sergeant."

"Ft. Bragg, sergeant."

And so they went. Three of them trained at Ft. Benning, one of the best infantry schools in the world; two of them at Ft. Bragg, another good place. One went to Ft. Dix, which was primarily basic training and not known for its advanced training. Two of them were training at the utter asshole of the army world – Ft. Polk, Louisiana. There, they used the swamps and the tropical growth to create Tigerland, one of the most realistic and best training grounds for Vietnam-bound grunts. One of the kids looked Japanese so I assumed he was from Hawaii or maybe the Philippines. I pointed to him.

"You, where are you from?"

"Havaii," he said, using the right pronounciation for an islander.

"OK, Havaii, you are going to be my back-up as we walk around this place, OK?"

"Yes, Duffy," he said with a smile.

"Good. Your job, your singular focus, your only purpose in life until we get back inside the wire is to keep my ass alive, you dig?"

"I dig, Sarge."

We needed another key assignment.

"You, Ft. Bragg, you grab the radio. Do you know what our call sign is?"

"No, sergeant."

"We're Crossbow, my good man, and I am Crossbow One-one. Here's our frequency for today's walk. Got that?"

He shook his head in affirmation, as he struggled to get the radio on his back.

"You are then Crossbow One-one India. Got that? If someone wants to talk to me, they want Crossbow One-one actual. If they don't want me and will talk to you, then you are to respond as One-one India. OK?"

The new guy shook his head that he understood.

"Who's going to carry the hog," I asked. Puzzled looks were all I got back. God, these guys were green.

"The machine gun? The M-60? The hog?"

No one moved. I pointed at one of the guys from Benning.

"What did you qualify on the machine gun?" I asked

"Marksman," he replied. That was the lowest level of qualification.

"Did anyone fire Expert?" I asked.

No hands went up.

"We must have at least one of you who fired Sharpshooter, don't we?"

Two hands went up, one of them from the guy who trained at Dix. He was bigger than the other guy so he became the machine gunner for the day. I pointed at the other guy.

"You're the assistant gunner, all right? You stay on his ass with the extra ammo he can't carry and if he needs more you gather it up, right?"

He nodded yes, but he didn't look very confident.

"Hey guys, we aren't going to Hanoi so relax a little. This will be a good exercise for you before you get assigned to a company.

"You've been trained so put the training to use. I'm going to be watching for your noise discipline and the way you pay attention to details out there. We're looking for anything out of the ordinary, OK?"

A hand went up and I acknowledged him.

"What's ordinary?" he asked.

I laughed a little. How the hell were these guys supposed to know what normal looked like?

"Good question, guy. Just let me know whenever anything catches your eye.

"Now check your ammo. Make sure you have at least ten magazines. We need a thousand rounds for the hog, which is why we call it a hog. The assistant gunner, the AG, will carry three hundred rounds and the gunner carries two hundred. You guys split up the rest.

"Everyone, carry two grenades and radio, you grab a smoke and I'll carry a smoke. Make sure you've got a lot of water. It is hot as hell today and you'll sweat a barrel-full just walking around the wire. We're going out about a click – a thousand meters to you FNGs. Then we'll do a sweep around the jungle to the southeast and then we'll close in closer to the wire surrounding the base.

"Everybody got the program? Good, let's go."

The first sergeant was good enough to get us a deuce and a half to truck us to the gate. No use getting all sweaty before we even started the mission. I decided we'd check out the area where Alpha popped their ambush first. We'd get the hard part done now and take an easy walk around the base after.

We got to the gate in a cloud of khaki colored dust. Everything was bleached brown: the road, the dirt and the foliage along the road. The dry season would do that to everything. I got off the truck and looked over our route. We would walk down a little slope and through three dried-up rice paddies. There was some light forest on the left, so I'd need some guys to walk flank on that side. On the right side, there was a slope up about twenty meters and it was covered with brush. I would put someone up at the top of the slope to see if he had better sightlines. "Havaii," the radio and I would go straight up the middle, through the paddies. Once through them, we would head farther south through some light jungle and then head west to start the lap around the base. A piece of cake, I thought. I was pointing all this out and checking to see if the guys were geared up when one of them pointed down to the paddies.

"Hey, Sarge, is that something that ain't ordinary?"

I looked down and saw the people who had been working in and around the paddies look at us and haul ass. They weren't running but they weren't hanging around either. It was a sign to me that they didn't want to be around when we got down there.

"That is exactly something that ain't ordinary," I said. "Something is going on down there and it ain't anything good."

I assigned the guys to cover the flanks and the top of the slope. I decided to put two guys on the slope instead of the one I'd originally assigned. I got that feeling that things were about to go south pretty quickly. But we weren't ten meters away from the base gate. How the fuck could things go wrong here?

"All right" I said, "let's move out."

As we started the descent toward the paddies, I brought the radio up and took the handset.

"Crossbow Six, this Bow One-one, over."

"One-one, go."

"We got some unusual activity down in these rice paddies and I'm getting a feeling the doo-doo is about to hit the rotary blades. Over."

"One-one, this is Crossbow Five. You aren't five minutes out and you got a problem? Over." Crossbow Five could have been anyone from a senior NCO to an officer with a nice rear job. His job was to monitor the radio and take down our periodic situation reports.

"Not yet, Five, but I don't like the looks of things, especially with a band of FNGs. Over"

We reached the start of the rice paddies, and I didn't want to be talking on the radio if anything happened.

"One-one, out." I handed the handset back to the radioman. He'd heard every word I said, of course, and he looked scared.

"Don't worry, kid. I'm just negative by nature." I smiled at him but that didn't help.

We looked good, I thought. The left flankers were out about fifty meters and looked wary. I thought that with the trees and brush on that side, whatever came at us would come from over there. We walked over the first paddy dike. I looked up the slope and saw our guys being very vigilant. Maybe what I saw didn't mean what I thought it meant. We had just reached the end of the second paddy when one of the new guys called down.

"Hey, Sarge, something's moving around down there," he said, pointing down the slope.

"Are you sure it isn't mama-san trying to gather up

her kids?" I asked.

"I don't know about no mama-san, Sarge, but something sure as hell is in that brush!"

"Come on, Havaii, we'll check it out."

We started walking toward the slope. I was convinced that there couldn't be any danger on this side as the slope was too thickly covered with brush and shrub to afford an exit strategy. What hell did this guy see, I asked myself and quickly found out.

A gook with an AK-47 jumped up from the brush. He wasn't ten feet away. He fired off three shots, all of them directed at Havaii. He never looked at me. I saw one of the rounds, a green tracer, rip through the Hawaiian kid before he fell into the dirt. Almost simultaneously, I squeezed off three rounds from my rifle, dropping the guy back into the brush. I hoped that it was over but as my uncle once said, "Shit in one hand and hope with the other and see which fills up first."

I heard the "whoosh" of the RPG as it left the launcher and watched it explode in the tree line. I found the shelter of the high dike separating the paddy from the slope and dropped down behind it. The good news was that I was defilade from anyone shooting at me from the slope. The bad news was I couldn't see anything beyond the top of the dike. So I pulled a grenade and yanked the pin. I lobbed it up where I thought I heard the rocket launcher. Before that one could explode, I pulled the pin on a second grenade and threw that up. The explosions kicked up a lot of twigs and dirt and debris. I was groping for another grenade when the radioman handed me one of his. He looked scared but he was composed. He had the handset to his ear and was chattering into it but he still knew I needed a grenade. Good kid, I thought. I pulled that pin and hooked it like a basketball shot into the brush. It exploded and I jumped up fearing another rocket grenade could be fired at my troops. I was on full automatic, spraying bullets into the brush. I yelled up to the guys atop the slope.

"See anything else? Give me eyes!"

I heard nothing in response so I went on. I saw the guy who shot my Hawaiian. He was holding his stomach while a shoulder wound was leaking blood into the brush. The guy who fired the rocket was trying to deal with the loss of much of his lower leg. One of the grenades must have landed pretty close to do that much damage. He was spurting blood from a couple of places. He'd be dead quickly. I reached down for the RPG launcher and when I did I heard a bullet zing over my head.

What the fuck? I wondered.

I dropped down behind the gook and reloaded. I started shooting blind, just squeezing off rounds all over the place. As I was shooting, I heard a voice from up the slope.

"One guy, twenty meters away. He's got an AK but he ain't shooting. He might be out of ammo."

Might, I thought, what a wonderful fucking word in this situation. I threw the grenade launcher a little to my right and waited for a response. Nothing. I started crawling on my hands and knees to the left. The brush was thick and I made a hell of a noise but no one was shooting. The bad guy was either waiting for me to get closer or he was indeed out of ammo. I moved about five more meters, getting my hands and face ripped by the brush and the vines and the brambles. I heard a noise so I hooked around a little to the right. I moved a branch out of the way and thought I was spending my last minute on earth. I was staring into the barrel of an AK. I could only wait for the shot that would take most of my head off. Then I saw the bastard pull the trigger and I heard the click of his empty rifle. I didn't hesitate. I fired two into his chest and knocked him backward. I took a minute to get over the experience of staring into the end of my life and composed myself.

Then everything was quiet. The air stunk with cordite and the nasty smell of blood but all I could hear was the buzzing of the flies feasting on the bloody corpses.

"Anybody see anything? Tell me what we've got!" I got no response.

Jesus Christ, I thought. This was supposed to be exercise. We're within five hundred meters of the fucking gate. I thought about the Hawaiian and made my way as quickly as I could through the tangled growth. The medic had stopped working on him. Bandage wrappers were all over the dusty paddy.

"Nothing I could do, Duffy," the doc said. "One of the rounds went through his chest and ripped the shit out of the area around his heart. I think he was dead before he hit the dirt."

"I saw one of the rounds, a green tracer, pass right through the poor kid," I said.

"That one went through his stomach, and if he was dead from the other bullet it saved him from a lot of pain," doc said.

"Fuck me," I said. "The kid wasn't here a fucking week and he buys it on my watch."

"What did you think you could do?" the doc said. "You didn't shoot him and you killed the guy who did."

"Not yet, doc. He's up in the brush and he was still alive when I left him."

"Still alive?" the doc said. "You run out of ammo or something?"

"Very funny," I said. "Let's see if he's still breathing."

While we made our way up the slope, an armored

personnel carrier was rolling down out of the base. The radioman came up and said he was getting calls asking if we needed air support.

"Now they fucking call," I said. "Tell them we have one friendly KIA and two or three enemy KIA. Negative on air support."

He started yapping into the radio while we made our way to the wounded NVA. He was still alive but probably wishing his wasn't. There was blood all over the place and he was looking ghostly pale. The doc hit him with a shot of morphine to case a little of the pain.

"He'll be gone in a minute," he said.

The radioman came up again.

"They want to know if it is two or three dead NVA," he said.

"Give me that fucking thing." I took the handset.

"This is One-one. We have two certain KIAs and one dying. So if you want to count him as half-dead and we can upgrade him to all the way in a minute or two."

"One-one, this is Five actual. Any chance of interrogating the wounded NVA?"

Interrogating, I thought, is that all they fucking care about? They want to interrogate a half-dead VC but didn't even mention the friendly KIA.

"No chance, Five. This guy is just about gone."

"Tell doc to try to keep him alive, One-one."

"Roger that," said. "One-one, out."

I looked at the doc still trying to work some magic on the poor NVA guy.

"They want to interrogate him, doc. Can we keep him alive until they get a crack at him?"

"Maybe. This is the toughest bastard I ever saw. He should have been dead ten minutes ago. If we get him medevac-ed quickly, a real doc might be able to work on him."

I looked at the radioman and told him to call in a medevac ASAP.

The armored personnel carrier pulled into the paddy and some of the GIs jumped off.

"Hey, Sarge," one of them said. "We ambushed these gook bastards last night so really, they are our kills."

"What?" I shouted. "All you're worried about are the kills? OK, guy, you can have the kills. Three of them and one of us. How's that? Make your fucking tally four for the day."

"What the fuck, Sarge? You going to blame us for one of yours getting wasted? How the fuck does that work?"

"The way it works, asshole, is that you let these guys get away last night. You didn't finish the job and today, my guy gets zapped because all you did was piss these guys off.

So you want three? You got to take four."

The arrival of the medevac chopper stopped me from really getting in that guy's face. They loaded the wounded NVA soldier and took the Hawaiian too.

"Hey Duffy," the doc said, what was that kid's name?"

"I have no fucking idea, doc. I never thought to ask him."

I did tell him his sole job was to keep me alive, I recalled. So what was my job? What was my sole purpose in life? I had no fucking idea anymore.

CHAPTER FIFTEEN

FIRST LIGHT AFTER A LONG NIGHT

We have to do what?" I said way too loud. "Are you shitting me? Why don't you go piss up a bent rope, LT"?

The skinny lieutenant looked stricken. I was challenging him in front of the platoon and that was a big-assed no-no.

"Piss up a bent rope?" he said, trying to lighten the mood. "Where'd a Yankee like you learn how to talk like a southerner?"

I was in no mood for levity.

"Don't change the subject, goddamn it! Why do I get every shitty job in this company, LT? You want to punish me, I'm OK with that but I have a dozen kids in this squad who don't deserve to be called out every goddamned time some officer gets a wild hair up his ass. When does the bullshit end?"

My little rant didn't make me feel any better and it only got worse when I saw the way the other guys were looking at the lieutenant. I knew it wasn't his fault, but who the fuck else could I yell at? To his credit, the LT stared right back at me and held his ground.

"Don't you even think about fucking with me Duffy. You've been in this army long enough to know shit rolls down hill. You got an order–a direct order–you take your squad out and retrieve the bodies.

"The bird leaves in one-zero minutes. If you hurry up and complete the mission we can get you back here before nightfall."

"There is no fucking way we can get this done and be back before nightfall, *Sir*! You know and so do I. So the plan is to strand me on that pimple for the night with just twelve guys…"

"Eleven," the lieutenant. interrupted. "One of your guys is staying back for guard duty."

"Beautiful," I said, "just fucking beautiful. So when we get whacked out there who are you going to send to pick up our bodies, Sir?"

I executed a perfect about-face for the first time in my

military career and headed back to my squad. My "crack soldiers" were competing for turns with a yo-yo that came in last week's care packages. Another guy was trading an orange Tootsie Pop for a cherry and two guys were scanning the latest Incredible Hulk comic book. I was now going to steal another strip of their youth with this bullshit mission.

"Quit the grab-ass," I barked. "Saddle up and head to the pad. We got us a mission. Travel light."

The lights in their collective eyes dimmed all at once but they started moving even as they bitched.

"Sarge, why they keep fucking with us? Are we the only squad in this company?"

"Shit, Sarge, where the hell we going this close to dark?"

"That's enough of the bullshit!" I said, slipping into my harness and checking my canteens. "Since when did this squad become a rat-fucking democracy? We're going because they told us to go. That's all you need to know."

"Now get your asses in gear. We got work to do!"

I led them to the helipad and squeezed in a quick briefing just ahead of the bird's prop wash.

"Observation chopper saw some bodies out near the Toilet."

The groans from the guys interrupted me.

"Listen the fuck up, assholes! We get dropped, we

collect the bodies and we get picked up and brought back here so I can tell you a bedtime story."

"They coming to get us at night, Sarge?" the radioman asked.

"No. We get it done and we get out. We ain't spending a night on that shitty piece of ground."

My words sounded convincing but I could see none of the guys bought it. Before they could protest further, the noise of the chopper drowned everything out. All that was left to do was jump on board.

As the bird sped off, I knew we were getting hung out to dry. There was no way we could do all that was required before dark. If we couldn't, it meant a night on a barren hilltop already soaked with a lot of blood from both sides. It got its nickname from the pilots who named it after dropping all kinds of ordinance on it.

"It's had so much shit thrown at it," a gunship pilot said, "it's got to be a toilet." And so it was.

The top of the hill was as bald as a monk. Napalm, artillery, high explosive bombs and aerial rockets had stripped, blasted and burned away all of the foliage from the hilltop. The last time we visited the Toilet we were locked in a two-hour battle against more gooks than I could count. Only the choppers and a bad-assed cargo plane turned gunship called Spooky kept us from being overrun. The next day, a squad from the third platoon went out to do a damage assessment. They never returned. We obviously hadn't done enough damage. Now, it was our job to bring them home.

Fifteen minutes later, we could see the Toilet. It rose above the surrounding jungle like a huge boil needing to be lanced. I started to get that gnawing feeling in my belly. I knew mine wasn't the only belly feeling it.

"Get ready to jump!" I screamed over the din of the chopper. "We ain't touching down!"

The helicopter raced to the top of the hill and hovered while we jumped from its safety into the unknown. As the chopper started off, one of the door gunners gave us a thumbs-up. The machine gunner replied by giving him the finger. Then, it was quiet, deathly quiet.

"Here's the deal, I said quickly. "I have the point. We're going down that side and I'll stay true to the compass bearing. We are going to move very fast. When we get to the bodies, we radio a chopper with a cargo net. We pop smoke, they lower the net and we load the bodies. Then we hustle back up here to get taken out.

"This is the part where I usually say 'any questions' but I don't give a rat's ass if you have questions this time. Just stay on the tail of the guy in front of you."

I finished the sentence already moving down the hill. I was moving very quickly, too quickly to be in any

sense secure from anybody with bad intentions. I was
virtually running down the hill. I felt the branches and
vines scratching my face and arms but I didn't care. I was
determined we were going to get this done before dark. I
might have made it too, except for the muck at the bottom
of the slope.

I smelled it before I saw it. When the rain came, it ran
down the hill and settled in the gulley between two slopes.
The jungle canopy stopped the sun from reaching down
to the floor and the water just sat and stagnated and stunk.
Trying to get through it was like wading in quicksand.
The mud sucked and grabbed and tugged at my boots. The
foul air under the canopy was as hot as it was stinking.
The sweat poured off my head and ran in a constant stream
down my face, stinging my eyes and salting my cracked
lips. Every step was combat against the mud and I cursed
all those who had anything to do with me being in this
cesspool. The light was fading fast when I looked to the
heavens and muttered:

"You're just trying to test me, aren't you?"

Every step I took sent a stream of stink upwards.
My lips and eyes burned and my nostrils kept telling me to
puke. This was getting way worse than I thought.

The radio guy appeared behind me. I had no clue how
he kept up with me carrying the radio and all but he was

right there with me.

"We got a bird hovering over the bodies," he told me. "They are going to drop some smoke to show us the way. They said they are laying about three hundred meters from the base of the Toilet."

"Three hundred meters??? It could take us the rest of the night to make it that far through this slop. I'm going to look for another way," I said. "Wait here."

I sank mid-calf in the mud with every step looking for drier ground. My legs were starting to cramp and the sweat steamed off of me. I fought the mud for about twenty meters before I hit pay dirt. And that's what it was, dirt. I pulled myself on to terra firma and waited for my trembling legs to settle down. I signaled to the radioman and he guided the rest of the squad to the new trail. When I was certain the guys knew the way, I just drove through the wait-a-minute vines and the other foliage like a fullback breaking arm tackles. I ducked under a low hanging branch and saw the twirling tendrils of smoke curling up from the jungle. I half crawled and half ran to the smoke. I shoved a thick bush from my face and was suddenly face to face with a hideous purple skull. It grinned at me like a wrinkled grape. The lips had shrunk from the mouth and revealed bright purple gums and violet streaked teeth. The skull scared the shit out me and it wasn't until the rest of the squad broke through the jungle that I got my composure back. The chopper had dropped the smoke grenade right next to the head of the corpse and dyed it in the purple haze.

"Smoke marked the spot, all right," the radioman said. "Look at that poor bastard."

"Look, my ass," I said. "We've got a job to do and a hill to scale. Let's get on it.

"Tell the bird with the sling to drop it so we can start loading."

I heard the radioman's singsong voice giving directions and soon after the rope net dropped. I directed four guys to set a loose perimeter and the rest to begin the grizzly task of putting the bodies, their parts, and assorted skulls into the net. The bodies were bloated and stank to the high heavens. More than once, a body simply came apart as it was being loaded into the net. We worked with the sound of the bird overhead and the buzzing of the flies all around the bodies. Leeches were everywhere. Stink was everywhere. And we were exhausted. But we got the bodies loaded with some sunlight still streaking the jungle.

"All right, guys, we did the dirty work now we get back up and out of this fucking sewer," I said, but the guys needed no encouragement. No one wanted to be stranded for the night on the Toilet. I took the point again and began the charge back up the hillside. Coming down was hard but nothing like going up. My heart threatened to beat right out of my chest. The muscles in my legs felt like they were soaked in gasoline and set on fire. Every instinct in my body told me to stop and rest before my body just shut down. But it wasn't a mission anymore. It was a test of my will, my strength and of me. I would not fail the test. So I drove myself on, running up the steep slope, willing myself to reach the summit in time for evacuation. I was about fifty meters from the summit when I convinced myself we were going to make it. There was enough daylight left and we would reach the top in time.

Goddamn, I thought, we're going to make it.

My lungs were about to explode when I reached the summit. I dropped to my knees and sucked in deep gulps of air. I motioned for the radio and held the handset while my heart slowed.

"Bones One Six, Bones One Six, this is Bones One One, over."

"Six, this is One Six, go."

"Six, mission-accomplished. We're at the rendezvous point ready for extraction, over."

"One One that's a negative. We're facing bad light conditions and can't risk a bird for the pick-up, over."

"What the fuck, One Six! The deal was we grab the meat and you grab us."

I look around the summit as the rest of the squad came over the top. They could tell I was agitated.

"One One … settle in and we'll get you at first light. Out."

Out, my ass you fucking scum bag. We're stuck here for the night on one of the bloodiest hilltops in our area and you cut me off with a simple "out?" Sonofabitch, someone's going to pay for this, I thought. That is, if we ever get out of here. I sat heavily in the dust, my sweat turning the slime on my pants into mud. I let the handset fall and looked at the last dazzling hold of the sun on the day. It wasn't going out gently. Rather, it blazed gold and red and purple, a brilliant black eye of a sunset hanging on to each second it could. Somewhere, I thought, that sunset would be deemed beautiful. Poets would write about it. Lovers would hug as it glowed. And here, we might die before we see another one. I watched the sun sinking lower behind the now shadowy mountains, haloing their outline with a deep indigo that would soon be black.

I signaled to the squad to form up on me but they didn't need words to hear the bad news. They read it on my face.

"We got fucked again, kiddies," I told them. "No bird tonight. So the good news is we don't have to dig holes. There are plenty all around the perimeter. The bad news is we don't have enough men to fill the holes. One man to a hole. We need 360 degree security so space yourselves to make sure we go all the way around the hill."

"Ah, Sarge, I don't mean to be the bearer of bad tidings," the machine gunner said, "but we're going to have so much room between us Mr. Charles could drive a truck between our holes."

"Well, let's all say a little prayer that Mr. Charles doesn't have any fucking trucks tonight. I know we're thin but this wasn't my idea so let's do the best we can and with any luck we might see the sun come up tomorrow."

We set out claymores and trip flares to cover some of the gaps between holes and I hoped that the bad guys couldn't see where we put them. There was no question that we'd been seen. The sound of the chopper landing on the hill would have alerted spotters all over the area to check on what the dumb-assed Americans were doing tonight. I hoped they would think it too preposterous to leave eleven guys all alone on the hill over night. If they didn't, it wouldn't be poets writing about the sunset but reporters writing our obituaries. I made a trip around the perimeter wishing there was something I could do or say to make this whole shitty episode go away. The men were as exhausted as I was but I knew they would be too scared to sleep. Fear can be a great motivator.

I tried to be quiet as I moved around the hilltop but every sound echoed like a base drum in a monastery. Convinced there was nothing more to do or say, I slunk into my hole and took off my watch. The last thing I needed was a reminder of how slowly this night would pass. I went through the night position ritual of laying out my bandoleers of ammo and straightening the pins on my grenades. Now, there was nothing to do but wait, either for the gooks or morning.

I settled in to my hole as the darkness became blackness. There was nothing quite as complete as the black of a jungle night. I held my hand up a foot from my face and could barely make its outline. In fifteen minutes, I wouldn't be able to see it at all. Unless someone tripped a flare, we'd never see the VC until they were slitting our throats.

I leaned against the wall of my foxhole and tried to calm down with the dirt against my face. It felt good and cool and I felt myself relax for the first time since the ordeal began. I was still stained with the blood from the bodies and caked in mud from the gully and soaked with sweat from the exertion that had all been in vain. I wanted to fight against the sleepiness I felt coming over me. I needed to be awake in case …

In case what? I wondered. We'd been left on this God-forsaken hilltop alone. If the VC came charging over the hill, we might kill a couple before we were overwhelmed and killed or worse yet, captured. I needed to be awake for that?

I guess the answer to that was no as I woke up lying in the bottom of the hole. I wanted to stand but something wouldn't let me. The blackness that surrounded me now had a crushing weight that sank against me, invisible but tangible. I tried to breathe but the night constricted my chest making it hard to get air. I was gasping, trying to get air into my mouth but the tightness in my chest wouldn't let me. I thought I was suffocating. I pushed up with arms but the weight was too heavy to move. I was pressed against the dirt, helpless and hopeless. The night was a living thing and using its weight to hold me fast against the bottom of the hole. I didn't know if my eyes were open or not. I didn't know if I was awake or dreaming. Blackness was all I could sense and feel. But it wasn't satisfied to just press down on me. It wrapped itself around me, slinking under me and squeezing me like an unseen snake. It flooded into my ears and nose and mouth, plugging everything. I no longer felt alive. I was simply existing--existing in a state that wasn't life but didn't feel like death. I was terrified and wanted to cry out but I couldn't make sound come out of my mouth. I felt the blackness wrapping around my skull and crawling into my brain. I was freezing but drenched in sweat. I had been scared before but this was a whole different dimension of fear. I felt icy fingers reaching into my chest and grabbing my heart. The pressure from outside was squeezing me like a cold rope wrapping around me. At the same time, something was inside me pushing out, like something wildly trying to escape. I had never been so terrified in my life but I could do nothing to fight back. I tried to struggle but was paralyzed by my fear. The blackness pushed and weighed and held me down so that simple movement put a desperate strain on me. I tried to get my arms to move, to push me off the floor, to do anything to resist this terrible threat to my sanity. But I couldn't. Nothing moved no matter how hard I strained. So I did the only thing left for me to do. I gave up. I stopped struggling and waited for whatever this was to consume me. I closed my eyes and waited to die.

I was still pressed against the floor of the foxhole but this time when I tried to move, everything was working. I sat up and saw the first shards of light streak the blackness of night. I lifted myself slowly still not sure that something wasn't lurking on the rim of my hole waiting to kill me. My muscles still felt tight but they all moved. I flexed my fingers and they worked too. What the fuck had happened? Did I dream that shit or was there something real that made me powerless to resist? I peeked over the rim of my hole. Nothing was stirring. No one was visible. The dawn continued to punch through the darkness and light came back to the world. The long black night was ending. Something else was ending as well. If I had been afforded a glimpse of death, it would hold no more fear for me. I'd faced my mortality in the darkness of my pit and shed my desperate fear of dying. I felt no fear as I climbed out the foxhole and called out to my troops.

"Rise and shine, Gents! It's time we got the hell out of Dodge."

I found the radioman in his hole and pulled out the radio.

"One Six, One Six, this is One One. Where's my fucking bird? Over."

"On the way, One One. On the way."

Heads popped out of the foxholes as the hilltop came back to life.

"Get some cover and blow your claymores," I ordered. "We don't know if Charlie snuck up and turned them around on us."

The shout went out for "fire in the hole" and the ball bearings shot out of the claymores, shredding tracts of the jungle.

I told the squad to gather up their shit for the ride home and was struck by how little talking there was. I didn't know if everyone had dealt with what I had during the night but something was definitely different. The day exploded in a brilliant, bright sunrise. One terrible night passed, another dreaded day to go. I sat on the edge of my hole and drank deeply from the tepid water in my canteen. I looked into the jungle and wondered exactly what the hell had gone on during the night. I closed my eyes and tried to recapture what the night had felt like but it was gone. I didn't know if that was good or bad. Years later and far from the inferno, the feeling would come back to me, recurring and terrifying. But then, I only knew that my heart ached where that something had grabbed me and that I'd been more terrified than ever in my life. (If that was death, it held no fear; but if this was life, it held no hope.)

I slung my ammo around my chest and drank again from my canteen as the thumping of the chopper's rotors came rising over the treetops. The heat of the early morning started me sweating again, thankful for the first light after the darkest night of my life.

CHAPTER SIXTEEN

THE INSULT

Thanksgiving already, I said to myself. Just a couple more months and my ass is gone from this bad motherfucker.

The lieutenant had given us the semi-good news a few minutes before. We'd be heading into the base for Thanksgiving dinner in the mess hall. The bad news was we wouldn't be staying back there. We would eat, burp and head back into the jungle. It sounded like a recipe for disaster to me: all these bloated grunts wandering through the weeds stuffed and sleepy. But what did I know? At least we'd be able to sit on chairs and at tables and eat like human beings for once. Little pleasures, I thought.

Before LT had given us the news, I'd been listening to the big man regale us with stories of his R&R in Sydney,

Australia. His name was Holcomb and he was a former tight end for one of those schools in Oregon, maybe the one with the Beavers for a mascot. At least he was until he was involved with one of his female teaching assistants who was delving into something deeper than macroeconomics. He was subsequently told his services were no longer required, nor was his presence on campus. I listened to him talk about round-eyed women with blond hair and blue eyes for ten minutes before I decided Sydney was the place for me, and I resolved to put in my own paperwork for rest and recuperation in the land Down Under.

Holcomb had come to us from some base in Germany where the spit-and-polish and regimentation of barracks life had driven him to volunteer for duty in Vietnam. I busted his ass about that for a solid week before he let me know he was tired of hearing about it and would not kick my ass till my nose bled if I would kindly end the harassment. I was OK with that. I didn't chirp about him being a volunteer and he didn't kick my ass. Sounded like a pretty good deal to me.

Holcomb led the second squad and I the first. He was a good guy and a better soldier.

"Hey, Sarge," my machine gunner snapped me out of my daydream about Aussie broads and beaches. "How long has it been since we've been back at base?"

I thought about it for a few seconds before realizing it had been a damned long time ago.

"Hell, from the smell of us, it's been about six or seven weeks." I said. "Way too long.

"All right! Get your shit tight. The birds will be here soon and I wouldn't want to leave any of you assholes back here."

After we packed up our gear, I told the radioman and the grenadier to burn all the paper we weren't taking with us. We didn't want package wrapping or envelopes with names on them falling into enemy hands. One never knew when Luke the Gook might use the cover of night and a name he'd found on a letter to lure someone out of a foxhole. It was something we did every time we broke a perimeter and moved on. But this time would soon become different.

We were in the middle of the dry season and the grass was brown and brittle. It took just one little puff of wind to carry a spark and within minutes, we were all fighting a grass fire that spread like, well, like wild fire. We got it under control just in time to see the helicopters coming over a distant tree line.

I got the guys into position to be able to jump on the choppers as quickly as possible. Extractions made the choppers vulnerable. They didn't like being on the ground too long as they made big targets for the VC. The grassfire left my face covered in ash and soot. I was still covered with it when we jumped aboard and rose rapidly away from the smoldering grass.

As much as I hated the chopper rides into the jungle, I loved these rides taking us out. The air was cool and the noise meant I didn't have to listen to anyone's bullshit. I was alone with my thoughts and my dreams. It was hard to believe that I was getting close to the end of this insanity. Sometimes it was hard to believe that I'd ever done anything else in my life. Other times, this all seemed like a bad dream. Pretty soon, I told myself, I'll be waking up from it.

From thirty-five hundred feet up, Vietnam could be seen as beautiful. The jungle boiled up in green balloons. We flew over some rice fields and the paddies looked geometric artwork. From up here, you could almost forget that the jungles and the paddies were full of death. I let the cool air dry my sweat and wash over me like a pleasant shower. I wished we could fly around for a few hours to help me forget about the true horror of this place. But much too soon, we could see the big base looming up in front of us. The long airstrip handled the big cargo planes as well as the choppers and our long line of birds stretched out along the runway, with their flared noses up, and touched down almost simultaneously. Thanksgiving was just a few hundred meters away now.

The birds took off in a blizzard of twigs and pebbles and we were left alone on the airstrip. My radioman signaled to me and pointed to the captain. So off I went eager to get our band of merry men into the mess hall.

"Squad leaders," the captain said, "get your men to at least give us a half-assed march to the mess hall. I don't want these rear echelon types to think we're just a band of cutthroats and pirates."

"But, sir," Holcomb said. "That's exactly what we are."

Everyone, including the captain, was laughing. Holidays will do that, I guess.

"I know that, sergeant," the captain said. "I just don't want anybody else to know it."

This captain replaced the other captain who was probably on the verge of getting assassinated by nurses that had to care for him after he got blown up. The new guy didn't act new and he was a pretty good guy, for an officer. He showed us some respect and we gave it back to him.

We hustled back to our squads and got them to pretend to be garrison soldiers for a while, and soon we were marching, mostly in step, along the oiled dirt road that would take us to the mess hall. Ten minutes and a left turn and we were there.

There was a trickle of guys heading in and out of the mess hall while we stood along the road. They were all spiffy in clean, starched fatigues and looked every bit soldiers. We, on the other hand, looked like we'd been in the jungle too long and had been putting out a grassfire–both of which were true. It seemed to be taking an inordinate amount of time for us to get into the building and out of the hot sun.

But what the hell, I thought. We're here and the food is right there. I sneaked a peek into one of the mess hall windows and saw how spiffy everything looked: the finest vinyl tablecloths accented with candle-stuffed Chianti bottles. I wondered how long it had taken the corpulent mess sergeant to drink all the wine to get the bottles ready for the candles. I also saw a guy eating something that looked like pie with ice cream on top – *ice cream*!

And still we were standing in the street, sweating our asses off. I saw that Holcomb was getting as antsy as I was and I gestured to him to see what the hold up was. He went forward and stood with the captain for a bit before being sent back to his squad. I walked over and asked what the hold up was.

"It seems that the fucking mess sergeant thinks us too dirty to eat in his 'dining hall.'"

"Dining hall?" I said. "Since when the fuck did this become anything besides a mess hall? And we're too dirty? Has that fat fuck looked in the mirror lately? He has had a lifelong estrangement from soap. It's a good thing the turkey smells so good. Otherwise, we'd be smelling his nasty ass."

"I think that captain is trying to make those same points with a little more tact than you have just used," the big man said, laughing.

We both look toward the 'dining hall' door and saw the battalion commander come out on the first step.

This isn't good, I thought. And it wasn't.

Our fate was sealed the moment the battalion CO put his arm around our captain. That is the surest sign in the world someone is about to get fucked.

"Bend over," I said to no one in particular. "Here it comes."

The pantomime continued with the colonel's grand gestures, the silent nodding of our caption and the smug, self-satisfied grins of the slovenly mess sergeant.

It went on so long, I wondered if we would eat at all.

But the captain returned to us looking every bit like he'd been kicked in the nuts.

"Well boys, we get to eat–just not in the mess hall," he said. "It seems like we're too dirty to eat with the rear echelon guys. So they will bring us our food."

"Where exactly are they going to bring it, sir?" I asked.

He hadn't told us where for a reason.

"We'll be served on the side of the airstrip," he said quietly.

"What was that, sir?" Holcomb yelled. "We can't hear you back here."

The big man had heard every syllable. He just wanted to yank the captain's chain a bit. But the captain had endured all the yanking he could.

"On the fucking runway, goddamn it! Now move out!"

The situation was rife for a mutiny. We'd been out in the jungle for more than a month. We'd been eating out of cans for all that time and drinking warm water to wash that crap down. We'd slept on the ground or in holes we had to dig. We were tired, scared, hungry, and dirty but we were soldiers, goddamn it, and we were too proud to be treated like fucking bums. But the big man must have said something funny because all the guys around him started laughing. Pretty soon the laughter spread to the entire company. I had no idea why but I was laughing too. The situation was too absurd to be taken seriously, I guess.

We dragged our dirty, tired butts back to the airstrip and sat ass-in-the-grass once more, this time to

eat Thanksgiving dinner. It arrived: hot and delicious and
plentiful. When we needed more, we radioed to the "dining
hall" and second and thirds were brought out to us. As
we sat there, laughing and burping and farting, I couldn't
imagine a better place for dinner. We were bonded by our
suffering and our continuing sacrifice and by the insult just
heaped on us. But we were bonded too by our camaraderie
and our abiding respect that only those who have suffered
together can know. So what if we had to lean over to shield
our plates each time a chopper or plane would land? So
what if arriving flights kicked up twigs and the stones all
kinds of junk we had to pull from our gravy? It wasn't so
much what or where we ate that Thanksgiving dinner, as it
was whom we ate it with.

When the sun was almost gone, it blazed a brilliant
red and gold goodbye in the western sky, we rose bloated
and somewhat happy to trek back into the jungle. As usual,
the first squad had the point and as usual, we bitched and
moaned about it all the way to perimeter barbed wire. I
looked around and noticed that Holcomb's second squad
was supposed to be behind me. They were there but there
was no big man. I asked his radioman where he was. He told
me he stayed behind on sick call.

What a fucking sham, I thought. He knows how much
he's needed in the bush. How could he stay behind after a

day of ups and downs like this?

But off we went, back to the jungle to give the VC another crack at us.

CHAPTER SEVENTEEN

CHANGE FOR CHANGE'S SAKE

Have you got a razor, Duffy?" the captain asked.
"Hell yeah, Six, and it's almost brand new," I
said, smiling. I hadn't shaved in a while and my beard was
flecked with dirt. I was starting to look scruffy.

"Clean yourself up and you can ride into the base with
me for the change of command ceremony," he said.

"Tell me you aren't leaving us, Six?"

"Hell no, Duffy. You're stuck with me for the
duration. Cold Steel Six, the battalion commander, is
rotating back to the States. We get to meet his replacement."

"Is the new guy any good?" I asked, afraid of the
answer.

"I don't know," the captain said, "but I heard this was
his first combat command."

Oh fuck, I thought, that doesn't sound good.

"We get to stay overnight?" I asked.

"Yes we do, sergeant, but there is a chopper on the way out so get your shit together before it arrives."

"That's a roger, sir." Hell yeah I'll shave to spend a night in the rear. Every night out of the bush was a good night. Ten minutes later, I was clean-shaven but still clad in my filthy and stinking fatigues. Fifteen minutes later the bird was in sight.

Hot damn, I thought, another night out of this craziness. I had no idea of the craziness that lay ahead.

The captain and I were all set to hop on the chopper when who should hop off but the Big John Holcomb himself. His stay in the rear on sick call was brief. I shouted to him over the noise of the helicopter.

"Not sick any more, asshole?" I asked with a grin.

"Nope, Duff, everything's just fine." His smile made me think he must have gotten laid but there were no whores allowed on the base. He looked at my smooth face.

"You shaved. You have a date or something?"

The captain and I jumped on and the bird whirled off, climbing quickly over the jungle and into the cool air we rarely got to feel. The ride back to the rear took about fifteen minutes and I used every one of them to think about how I'd be out of this insane asylum and back in the World in a little over a month. And part of that month would be spent in Sydney-goddamned-Australia where the women had round eyes and the bartenders didn't try to cheat you. A-fucking-men to that.

We were no sooner on the ground at the base than the captain took a sniff and scowled at me.

"You stink, Duffy. You can't go to the change of command ceremony smelling like a horse been rode hard and put away wet. Go over to supply, get some clean fatigues and find some place to take a shower. You got fifteen minutes before we report to see the new battalion CO."

I set off to make myself look presentable smiling to myself because I thought it was the captain stinking up the chopper. I got to the supply room and for the first time in months got a set of fatigues that actually fit. The sergeant there wanted to give me brand new ones but I was afraid the shine of new duds would make me look like a FNG.

"Sarge, I need some that looked lived in, not some that look like I've been fucking around in the rear with you."

He scowled at me but complied, and I headed off to find a usable shower.

I got back to the battalion command post with about two minutes to spare.

"You look almost human, Duffy," the captain said. "I thought we were going to start without you."

I just smiled and took in the sweet smell of burning shit that always reminded you that you were on the base.

Not that I had all that much interaction with a battalion commander but I was sorry to see this one go. I'd spent some time on the ground with him when we got left behind with a few dozen other grunts and we spent the night blowing up a bunch of gooks that didn't know we were still there. He got the Silver Star, I heard. I got a couple pairs of clean socks and an "attaboy" from him.

I didn't like the looks of the new CO. He was pasty faced and looked like someone transplanted from the World and he had the shape of the Pillsbury Dough Boy, whereas the departing colonel looked like a soldier. But I stood at attention and went through the motions as the battalion flag was passed around and salutes were exchanged. When the formalities ended I had every intention of heading off to the enlisted man's club and hammering down some cold beer but that didn't happen.

"Stick around, Duffy," the captain said. "The new CO wants to see us."

"Us?" I said. "Why 'us' and not just you?"

"He wanted me to bring one of our better NCOs in for the briefing."

"Aw shit, sir, I didn't know you cared."

"Save the bullshit for later, sergeant. I don't think this is a 'meet-and-greet.'"

"Roger that, sir," I said. "I'll pull up my serious drawers."

"Yeah, right," the captain said. "You haven't worn 'drawers' since you got here."

"I know," I said. "They chaff the shit out of my thighs and …"

"Okay, Duffy, I don't need more detail than that. We've got about thirty minutes before the meet so stick around."

I killed the time shooting the shit with some of the guys who'd been lucky enough to get jobs in the rear. I wondered if time passed as slowly for them as it did out in the bush. It wasn't long before I saw the captain emerge from the company headquarters and give me the nod so off I went to see the wizard.

We were ushered into the battalion commander's office as soon as we arrived. I wondered if punctual also meant competent. I was not a big fan of change. Change usually resulted in something bad happening. There were sounds in the jungle that you expected to hear. When the sounds changed, the shit usually hit the fan. When we were headed in one direction and the order was given to change direction, the shit usually hit the fan. When we traveled by truck and the road was all one color except for that certain patch ahead, it usually meant that the shit could hit the fan. Now our leadership changed, I was praying that this would be the exception to the change rule.

The rotund lieutenant colonel didn't stand when we entered the room. The captain centered himself on the commander's desk and saluted smartly. The colonel managed only a cursory wave of the hand that I assumed was his version of a salute. I was planted, as per military requirements, a step to the left of the captain and one step behind him.

"You must be Sergeant Duffy," the colonel said looking past the captain. "I understand from my predecessor that you've developed some sort of tactic that is resulting in high body counts."

"Sir, most of the credit goes to Cold Steel Six, I mean the old Cold Steel Six," I said. I might not have known much about the army but I knew enough to credit officers for good results.

"No need for false modesty here, sergeant," he said. "You have been recognized by your chain of command and that speaks volumes about your battlefield acumen."

Now I have acumen? I mused.

"Well, we are going to need all the acumen we can

scare up among your soldiers, captain," the new Six said. "Take your seats by the window and we'll get started."

An orderly entered and announced the arrival of Bayonet Six. I had heard a lot about this guy and his scouts. They flew all over our AO, searched for the bad guys, sometimes in platoon size and sometimes smaller. It took big balls to do that on a daily basis. We were all stationed along the super highway the VC and NVA used to travel from their safe havens in Cambodia to Saigon. We had a bad habit of interdicting them on an all too frequent basis. That did not make Luke the Gook happy.

A tall, athletic-looking guy came into the room, advanced to the proper three paces before CO's desk and saluted smartly. Again, it was returned with a half-assed wave of the hand.

"Go over to the map, captain and tell us what your scouts encountered yesterday." A giant six-foot-by-six-foot map of our area dominated one wall of the office.

"Sir, we had two birds carrying a total of sixteen troops, patrolling about four kilometers from the Cambodian border right about here," Bayonet Six said, pointing to an area not far from a night position we'd set up just before Thanksgiving. "They had been on patrol for about three-zero minutes when they spotted movement on the ground about here and went down to investigate.

"They saw a column of enemy soldiers moving northeast, roughly along this route of march. As my scouts got closer, they saw that the enemy had with them a recoilless rifle."

A recoilless rifle? I thought, that's way too big a weapon for even an NVA company to have. There must be a ton of fucking gooks out there.

Bayonet Six went on.

"One of our scout birds landed and set up a hasty ambush. They then engaged the enemy with small arms and machine gun fire. They were supported by the guns and rockets on the second chopper. When the shooting stopped we had seven enemy KIA, including one wearing the North Vietnamese rank equivalent to our colonel. We also captured the recoilless rifle."

They got a fucking colonel, I said to myself. There are more than a ton of gooks out there.

"Excellent work, captain," the colonel said. "Pass along my compliments to your scouts on a job well done."

"Thank you, sir," Bayonet Six said. "I'll be sure to tell my troops."

The pudgy little colonel put his hands together and spoke to us.

"That summarizes what happened in the past," he said "but you have been called here to discuss what will take place in the future. I'd like to hear your ideas about how we address this apparently large troop formation in our area of operation."

I took this as a good omen. He was willing to solicit opinions from leaders who have been in the field.

He looked at my captain who spoke up quickly.

"Sir, if the scouts took down a colonel and a recoilless rifle, it is a clear indication of a much bigger concentration of force than we've encountered before. So my recommendation is a B-52 strike to decimate the force and the designation of two rifle companies to go in and do a BDA (bomb damage assessment)."

Without being asked, Bayonet Six offered his concurrence.

"Bones Six has offered the right solution, sir," he added. "My scouts reported that the soldiers they killed were wearing fresh uniforms and were well armed. The riflemen carried 100 rounds of ammunition for their AK-47s. This would indicate a well-stocked, well-prepared regimental sized unit getting ready to inflict some damage. The heavy bombing suggestion makes all the sense in the world."

The colonel leaned back in his chair with his hands folded across his belly. He spoke with a smug smile on his face and I knew what followed wouldn't be good.

"Well prepared, you say? Then how did they allow such a high ranking officer and a large and an almost irreplaceable weapon to be taken?" the colonel asked. "We've cut off the head of this snake and now all that remains is to go in and finish the job. A B-52 strike would be like killing a fly with a shotgun. So instead, we're going to use this opportunity to establish the reputation of this command as being the 'go to' unit in the battalion. We're going to demonstrate what the fighting capabilities of this battalion are and we are going to smash this enemy force using organic weapons and resources."

I couldn't understand this all-consuming aversion of the brass to use bombs. I wondered if they might be paying for them. We had complete control of the air, lots of ways to drop bombs and lots of pilots who liked to drop them. So what's the deal with skipping the bombs to use bodies?

My stomach started churning. How could this dumb fuck pass up the opportunity to use the might of a B-52 bomber strike to blow these bastards away? I had seen stupid in my life, much of it perpetrated by me. But when I did it, no one got hurt but me. This prick was going to get good soldiers killed on a bad mission. I started to say something, which was absolutely taboo, but the captain lightly punched my thigh. Then, apparently reading my mind, he spoke.

"Sir, it is not unthinkable to assume that if this enemy force had one heavy weapon, they have more. I believe the prudent thing is to make that assumption and not unduly risk the lives of a rifle company or two when we have indirect resources that could be brought to bear with far less risk."

"If I didn't know the reputation of your company, captain, I'd say you're expressing a hesitancy to engage the enemy," the colonel said. "But I do know your reputation and that's why I'm designating you and your men to be the spearhead of my plan." He walked to the map.

"Thirty-six hours from now, you'll be air assaulted into this landing zone," he said, using a pointer to illustrate the spot.

Bayonet Six spoke up.

"May we approach the map, sir?"

"Of course, gentlemen. Come closer."

As I moved toward the map, I wondered what the penalty would be for killing this fat fuck and saving a bunch of lives as a result.

The scout captain pointed to a spot about a thousand meters from the end of the colonel's pointer. As he did, I wondered if that pointer would fit up the colonel's ass.

"This is where we made contact," he said, speaking directly to my captain. "When we saw them, they looked like they were heading away from this stream here to the south. My guys concluded they might be based somewhere in this portion of jungle to the north.

"If that conclusion is correct, sir," he went on, now speaking directly to the colonel, "that would put a landing at your designated spot dangerously close to the suspected enemy concentration."

I was staring at the map, hardly hearing the discussion. I knew we'd be fucked already but there was no sense expecting a kiss from the colonel to go along with the screwing. We would be coming in from the east heading west toward twin hills that hung down like two saggy tits. I was thinking about what I saw but didn't realize I was thinking out aloud.

"At least get us closer to this high ground to the west."

The discussion suddenly went quiet. All three officers were looking at me.

"What was that, sergeant?" the colonel said, emphasizing the 'sergeant.'

"Sir, as long as we are going to be sent into this area we know is enemy occupied," I said, "the strategic move would be to get us closer to these two hills, which would be easier ground to hold and defend."

"Interesting observation, sergeant, but we'll stick to the plan I've already set in motion," the colonel said. That was lieutenant colonel-speak for "keep your stupid ideas to yourself." He looked at my captain again.

"Bones Six and his company will land here," he said, putting the landing zone right between the stream and the thick jungle. "We will have two more rifle companies ready to reinforce if and when you make contact. You won't be alone, captain. You find the enemy and we'll pile on."

That's a great plan, I thought, as long as you aren't the bait. Too often, the bait is consumed before the fish is caught. I've got to get the fuck out of here. There are too many assholes trying to get me killed.

The colonel retracted his spiffy pointer, signaling to us that the meeting was over.

"Happy hunting, gentlemen," he said as we made for the door. We were only slightly out of his office when I spoke.

"Happy hunting, my ass. We're being hunted on this one."

The captain grabbed my arm.

"Not here, not now," he whispered, but I'd already said my piece.

We were heading back toward our company area when I smelled the odor of burnt wood. We detoured to find the source of the smell. We went along a path between two buildings and saw the smoking ruins of a building, but not just any building. The captain guided me between a couple of buildings and there lay the smoldering ruins where we'd been so rudely treated the day before.

"Wow, karma is a bitch huh?" I said. Then I remembered that Big John had spent the night back here.

No wonder he was smiling when he came back to bush.

CHAPTER EIGHTEEN

THE WISEST

H e's putting you where?" my new friend asked "Right in the middle of a shit storm is where," I said. We were both killing time at the bar at the enlisted men's club when we started talking about the new battalion CO. My new buddy was a scout, one of the very same scouts that had caught the gooks out in the open a day ago. So I asked him about the assessment they had made from yesterday's mission.

"Man, I was never so happy to get out of Dodge after we killed those guys," he said. "You know how you can just feel the gooks around you? That's what we were all feeling. Made the hair on the back of my neck stand up. I think what saved us was how quick we did those bastards in. Our Six is a smart motherfucker. He had us drop about half a klick away and set up a quick ambush while the other bird started herding the gooks toward us with their mini-guns. By the time they ran up on us, they were toast."

"But you think there were more out there?"

"Abso-fucking-lutely," he said. "You know the normal gook ain't humping no recoilless rifle. That's crew-served, man. Takes at least two guys just to carry it and a bunch more to carry ammo for it. And one of the guys we wasted was a colonel or some shit. I don't know what those guys were doing out there but they sure as hell weren't alone. Even our captain was nervous about getting in and out."

"Your CO was a stand-up in our meeting with the new battalion guy," I said. "He backed my captain's play for the B-52 strike, lot of good that did."

"Did anyone mention artillery support in your meet?" the scout asked.

"Not a fucking word," I said. "Why? That going to be an issue?"

"No ... no issue at all," he replied. "'Cuz you won't have any."

"What the fuck are you talking about? How could they send us out without artillery support?"

"When we went out on the scout mission, the captain told us we wouldn't be too anxious for a fight because the patrol area was outside the arty fan."

"What arty fan?" I asked. This mission was getting more fucked up by the minute. "Where are the closest guns?"

"Right here, man. Right here on the base. This is the closest and all they got here is 105s. They can only shoot about 30 miles. You better check where you're going because our captain said we were patrolling outside the range of the guns. It's not a great feeling knowing we're out there on our own."

"Your captain told you this?" I asked.

"Yeah, and so did the chopper pilot after we got back. He was a little nervous putting us down and picking us up without artillery back-up."

"Bartender! Give us a couple more. I don't know when I'll get another chance to have a taste," I said. "You got any advice for me about the mission?"

"Yeah, I got some advice," he said, taking a long drink out of the can. "Go on sick call."

The next morning, I made it to the chopper pad in plenty of time to meet the captain and fly back out to the bush. I had at least fifteen seconds to spare.

"Jesus, Duffy" the captain said. "You look like twenty miles of bad road. You look worse than yesterday."

"No sweat, Six," I said. "I don't need to be pretty to

get killed."

For the next five minutes I shared the input I got from the scout at the bar.

"You sure we won't have artillery support?" he asked.

"Fuck no I ain't sure," I said. "I don't know the coordinates of the landing zone and besides, isn't all that something you're supposed to know?"

The look I got from the captain told me I was rapidly losing his good will.

"Besides, if you had listened to me and got hammered with me, you could have heard all this stuff for yourself. Just check the coordinates of the LZ and see if we're landing more than five klicks away because five klicks is about as far as these 105s can fire."

"Good God, what is this asshole trying to do to us?" the captain said.

"It's pretty obvious to me he doesn't give two shits about what they do to us, Six. This guy was talking about the reputation of *his* battalion. Why did they relieve the other guy anyway? He was at least mostly a soldier."

"Officers get moved a lot, Duffy, especially field grade officers. A combat command is an essential for promotion so the army shuffles a lot of guys in and out of commands like the battalion. It's one more ticket that gets punched on the way to promotion."

"Why don't they use the same system they do for NCOs? I got promoted because somebody got hit."

The captain just smirked and changed the subject.

"Too bad about the mess hall burning down, huh? If you weren't with me the whole time, I'd have bet you did it."

"Me? I wouldn't have waited, Six," I said. "I'd have burned the fucking place down with the mess sergeant in it."

I was only half kidding. But I smiled nonetheless when I thought about who did burn the place down.

The chopper ride back to the bush was not as calming as the ride in had been. My stomach was churning with all the stale beer still in there. My mouth felt like it was stuffed with tennis balls. And my mind was trying to distill all the nonsense I'd heard from the FNG battalion commander. Three fucking days on the job and now it's *his* battalion.

I knew my next ride on a helicopter could be my last. I tried to rationalize our mission but I couldn't come up with anything but a suicide mission. We were going to be bait for a large, heavily armed force in an area too far away to get artillery support. What could possibly go wrong? I thought. Did anyone but me realize the bait usually gets eaten?

We jumped off the chopper at the company perimeter and when he could be heard the captain grabbed my shoulder.

"I'm going to brief the platoon leaders about the mission, Duffy, but I don't want the troops to know the whole situation. We could land and not find anything so don't get the men worked up for nothing."

I looked at the captain and knew he was full of shit about landing without consequences. He knew it too. I could see it in his eyes.

"Can you get on the horn and find out about artillery support?" I asked. "We shouldn't be out there with our asses hanging in the breeze."

"I'll do that before the briefing but don't spook the men with any of this. Do you understand?"

"Yes, sir. I understand."

By the time I reached my squad, they had all heard about the "tragic" fire back at the base. They were all grinning and bullshitting about it.

"Hey, Sarge, did you get to see the remains?" the machine gunner asked.

"See it? I smelled it as soon as I got off the bird. At first though, I couldn't tell if there had been a fire or the mess sergeant was making his specialty--burnt meat loaf."

That got them laughing but I knew I had to change the mood.

"We're going to take a little helicopter ride tomorrow,

gentlemen. So clean your weapons and stock up on ammo. Each rifle should have two hundred rounds and the hogs two thousand."

That was almost double the normal load so I got all the grief in response.

"Where the fuck we going, Sarge. Hanoi?"

"Not yet. We still have some VC ass to kick here. So knock off the bullshit and get yourselves ready. We got work to do."

I walked off to find Holcomb and ask him about the fire but the medic stopped me.

"How about me?" he asked.

"How about you what?" I said.

I was always amazed by the bravery of this guy and his ability to patch us up. When I talked to the other squad leaders they all said the same thing about their docs. These guys were a different breed.

"What do you want me to say, doc? I got a funny feeling about this one so if I were you I'd pack all the shit you can carry."

"That's what I thought," the doc said. "You say a lot when you don't use a lot of words."

"Is that a compliment?" I asked.

"Yeah, I guess it is, Duffy."

"Thanks. Now get your ass back over there and pack

your shit," I said, smiling.

Then I set off again to find Big John. He was loading some magazines with a dark scowl on his face.

"Hey, big man, why the long face? You don't look like the hero of the great mess hall fire when you frown."

That brought a hint of a smile.

"You should have been there, Duff. What a fucking site, watching that shit hole burn. Maybe they'll think twice about who they let in the next time."

"Well, you are the campus hero for that caper, my man."

The scowl returned.

"What the fuck is going on? My lieutenant just came back from a pow-wow with Six and started barking orders like we were in boot camp."

"We're taking a ride tomorrow and we're headed into Indian country. So pack heavy and make sure your weapon works."

"That's pretty much what the lieutenant said. What do you know that you ain't telling me?"

"I'm not supposed to say anything but we're probably going to hit the shit tomorrow. The scouts found a pretty big group of bad guys and we're going into that area to see if we can get some more."

"Fuck that shit!" he said. "Why is it always us? We

get all the shit jobs and the better we do at them, the more we get."

"That, my friend, is the eternal question," I said. "Let me know if you ever find the answer. But this one looks and sounds bad so we got no choice as to how we handle it. Let's just get this done. We get this one done and I'm off to Sydney.

"Besides, you are the big man on campus now. The guys all look up to you."

We laughed a little but the concern that I saw in the big man's face was probably just a reflection of what he saw in mine.

CHAPTER NINETEEN

WHEN IT HITS THE FAN

You can bullshit the average grunt just so far
Even the dullest dullard will catch on that
something special is happening when he sees machine
gunners strapped like Poncho Villa and their assistant
gunners carrying ammo cans. So when the order came to
police up our area and get rid of garbage, everyone knew
that this wasn't going to be just another day in Hell. After
our Thanksgiving morning fiasco with the grassfire, I was
especially careful about burning our stuff. Still, even our
little trash fire almost got out of control. Water was too
valuable to waste putting out a fire so I had some guys with
shovels ready to throw dirt if and when the fire extended
beyond the confines of the little hole we'd dug.

"Man, this grass is like paper," the radioman said.

"This shit so dry it'll turn to dust when you walk on it."

"Damn straight," the machine gunner chimed in. "How goddamned hot is it this morning, Sarge?"

"What difference does it make?" I said. "Isn't it enough that is it's *too* fucking hot for this early in the morning? We're sweating our asses off and it isn't oh-nine-hundred yet. This is going to be a long fucking day."

We'd been briefed at first light. The first platoon, as usual, would go out on the first lift. We had five birds assigned to the mission and each bird would carry eight grunts. When they dropped us off, they would head back to pick up another load. So the first guys on the ground were alone against whatever was out there. That made you get real serious real fast. It would take about ninety minutes to get the entire company ferried into the landing zone. My job was to take my squad out to the tree line on the east. It would be a hike of about five hundred meters. Knowing what I'd learned yesterday, I thought that would be the most likely place for the bad guys to be. But feeling the heat of the day already, I started thinking it might not be bad to be in the shade and be excused from digging in to the dry season ground now baked to hardness like concrete. Holcomb's second squad would deploy to the west along the creek. The third squad would head north toward the hills I'd dubbed "The Tits." Our job was to secure the LZ for the subsequent lifts. But it would be a lonely twenty minutes or so until the second lift came in.

As we broke up from the briefing, I caught the captain's attention.

"Any word on that artillery we're not supposed to have?" I asked.

"Battalion says the 105s can reach us but they were laying in more gunships than usual for support, just in case."

Just in case, my ass, I thought as I walked away. I'm numerically illiterate and I know you can't make a gun with a range of seven miles support a position nine miles away. I hoped those helicopter jockeys knew what we're likely to find today.

I walked passed the big man as he was herding his troops into position to board the helicopter from both sides.

"If you get killed today, can I have your water?" I asked. That was our equivalent of "break a leg" to an actor.

"Fuck you, Duffy. If you get wasted, I'm going to find your girlfriend." That was the usual retort. Seeing as how I didn't have a girlfriend, I thought I won that exchange.

I got back to my squad just in time to hear the radiomen shouting that the birds were inbound. A quick count of my men didn't add up. I was missing someone.

"Who's not here?" I yelled.

"The Texas twerp," someone answered. The Texas

twerp was a little douche bag who told everyone he was going to be the Vietnam War's Audie Murphy when in actuality he couldn't make a patch on the ass of Murphy's fatigues. He had a big mouth and an empty skull and everyone hated him. Later in life, I heard a phrase that fit him perfectly: "all hat, no cattle."

"Where the fuck is he?" I shouted.

"He went into the woods to take a shit," was the answer.

"Motherfucker, I'm going to kill that kid!" I yelled, heading for the wood line.

"Audie Murphy! Get your fucking ass out here" I screamed.

"Coming, Sarge" he said, running out of the trees.

"Get your ass over here and get ready to deploy, soldier!" I screamed.

He ran over to his rucksack and started pushing shit into it.

"You aren't even packed yet?" I yelled. "What the fuck is wrong with you, shithead?"

I helped him, throwing what little he had into the rucksack just as the choppers came over the tree line.

"Grab your rifle, asshole!" I said, continuing to pack his rucksack, "and pull up your goddamned pants!" I was still packing him when the flight touched down. I literally threw the little bastard onto to the deck of the bird and chucked his pack in behind him – just in time for the flight to lift off, leaving me stranded on the ground.

"Goddamn it!" I yelled into the rotor wash of the departing choppers. I ran back to the headquarters group and told the captain what had happened.

"What the hell, Duffy!" he yelled. "No one would have missed your soldier on the ground but you were supposed to be out there leading. Sonofabitch!"

I had not seen the captain that pissed before and had rarely seen him mad at me.

"You go out on the last lift, with the weapons squad," he said. "These squads followed orders and we're not going to break them up just for you."

So I waited until it was just me and the mortars and their ammo. I was listening to the radio reports coming from the landing zone and the designation was "green." That meant no enemy fire.

Thank God for small favors, I thought. On the flight to the LZ, I was thinking about reprisals against the Texas twerp. But as mad as I was, I knew that the captain was right. Who cared if the kid had been left behind? It was my job to get out there and provide security. I was the one who fucked up. I was the one who let my kindness become my weakness. The old Sarge was still haunting me.

We got in sight of the landing zone and troops were moving all over the place, digging in, stacking c-ration boxes and extra ammo. We were coming in from the south and I saw something that wasn't on the map. There was a dry gully running from the jungle to the east right by the southern limit of our perimeter. It looked deep enough that soldiers coming down the gully might do so unseen by troops in the perimeter. I made a mental note to alert someone to that danger. But mental notes would have to wait. As the bird began its descent I saw my squad laying around the LZ instead of being out on patrol. I jumped off the chopper and ran to my guys.

"Get the fuck up and start acting like soldiers!" I kicked the bottom of the machine gunner's boot for effect.

"Get up!" I said, "goddamn it! Our side of the LZ has no observation post! That's where we were supposed to be, so get your asses in gear."

The squad was on its feet when the grenade guy spoke.

"Hey Sarge, you're the leader. Don't blame us because you missed the bird."

I was as close as I ever came to shooting a GI at that point. He was right, but that didn't mean I wouldn't shoot him. I calmed myself a little to calm them and said evenly:

"All right, men. We head for that tree line. Twerp, you

take point. Bravo team, you're next, then me and the radio and doc, then Alpha team. Move out."

The twerp started to say something but the grenade guy pushed him forward and we started to move.

I signaled to the radioman for the handset and called into the captain to let him know we were moving. As I talked, I choked on the dust that we kicked up in the brown and brittle grass. I started to tell the captain about the gully but he stopped me in mid-sentence.

"I saw the damned gully, sergeant." He only called me "sergeant" when he was pissed. "Now kindly take up the position you were assigned. Out."

Well, what the fuck? I thought. He's still pissed? I'm here, we're moving, what the fuck else does he want?

The farther we walked, the higher the grass got. It was thigh high when we were about three hundred meters from the trees. I paused the march and went to front of the column.

"You see anything yet, dickhead?" I asked the twerp.

"Naw, Sarge, but I think somebody else took our place out there," he said pointing to the trees.

I looked where he pointed and saw the beginning of a very bad day. The guys he thought "took our place" were North Vietnamese soldiers scurrying around getting their shit together to attack. They let us land the whole company before they were going to hit us. They wanted us all on the ground, not just a few. That meant they knew they could beat us. The shit storm I feared was about to start. I had to get my guys back to the perimeter without letting the bad guys know we were on to them. Otherwise, we'd be sitting ducks in the crossfire between the perimeter and the jungle. I motioned to the radioman and took the handset when he approached. As I did, I heard him mutter "oh my God," as he saw what I saw.

"Bones Six, this is Bones One-One. We have a large enemy force massing in the tree line to my front," I said without waiting for any acknowledgement. "We're heading back toward the perimeter. Over"

"One-one, this is six. How many is a large force? Over."

"Six, one-one, too many to count but at least one-zero-zero. Over."

"OK, one-one, we're on alert, now get your butts back in here. Out."

"Roger that, six, we're on the move."

"All right, everyone just turn around and start back toward the LZ. I'll stay and cover the rear. Move out."

"Them's gooks, Sarge?" the twerp said, pointing to the trees. Then he switched his M-16 to full automatic and fired an entire magazine at the trees. That act switched our unofficial status from "cautious" to "fucked."

The blizzard of bullets that came from the tree line was stunning. Before I hit the ground I heard at least two bullets rip past my head. The twerp didn't react so quickly. He was virtually cut in half by all the rounds that hit him. The machine gunner screamed so I assumed he was hit. The radioman was next to me. He reached out to hand me the radio handset. Six was screaming into my ear.

"What the fuck happened, Duffy?"

"Just what we thought would happen. The battle started, sir."

"Jesus, we've no holes, no fighting positions, no..."

"We'll buy some time out here and hold them off while you get organized, and while you're at it, starting throwing some mortar rounds into the trees!"

We'd all been shot at before but nothing like this. The bullets sounded like a swarm of pissed off bees. They sawed the top of the dry grass off like a scythe and that grass was all we had for concealment.

"Get that hog firing!" I screamed over the din. "Put rounds in the trees. I don't care where! Just start fucking shooting!"

I heard the thump of the grenade launcher sending 40mm grenades toward the trees. Some rifle fire was heard but the guys were pinned to the ground by the storm of bullets coming from the NVA.

"Where the fuck is that machine gun?" I yelled. "Open up on the trees!"

I got no response so I assumed the worst. The gunner was down. I started crawling back to where I last saw the gun. That put a lot of strain on the radioman because he had to go where I went and no one wanted to go anywhere with the bullets flying overhead. I wondered how long it would be before the bad guys figured out they should be lowering the aim. When I reached the gun, the worst was confirmed. The gunner had taken a round that went into his shoulder and shattered his shoulder blade on the way out. The medic was on him and trying to stop the bleeding but the machine gunner was in a world of pain. I took the gun and a belt of bullets. I signaled to the radioman to grab a can of machine gun ammo that lay next to the gunner. So he had to carry the radio and drag the ammo as we crawled away from the wounded soldier and the medic. Once the machine gun opened up it would draw a lot of attention from the NVA. Crawling through the dry grass was a bitch. The gun weighed over twenty pounds. But that wasn't the worst of it. The grass broke off as I made my way through it and kicked up all the dust that had coated the stalks in the dry season. Every time I opened my mouth to suck in some air, I got the dust along with it. We made it about twenty meters when I'd had enough. I was choking on the dust and my sweat was turning into paste.

"Fuck it," I said. "We set up right here."

I lifted the cover off the feed tray and snapped in a long belt of the ammo. I didn't even have time to set up the bipod legs as we needed to get some fire into those trees. I was still waiting to hear the mortar rounds that would help suppress the enemy fire. But that was someone else's issue.

I held the gun just high enough to be effective and still keep my ass down.

The gun jerked against my shoulder as I squeezed the trigger. I fired short bursts but I didn't know if we could find all the ammo for the gun, and between the radioman and me we had about seven hundred rounds. The M-60 could fire almost all of that in a minute.

I fired another short burst before the radioman handed me the handset again.

Now what? I thought, doesn't this guy know we're in a battle?

"One-one go!" I shouted before ripping off another five round burst.

"We're getting ripped up in the perimeter, One-One! Can you see anything?"

"I lift my head, Six, I lose it. I'm firing the pig blind! Where are those mortars?"

"One tube took a .51 cal through it. We're trying to set the other one up. Over."

Jesus, the gooks had a .51 caliber machine gun? It fired a bullet almost four inches long and half an inch around. They were lethal on the ground but were just as lethal shooting at aircraft. One of their bullets pierced one of our two mortar tubes, rendering it useless.

"One-one, Silver Saber wants an update!" Silver Saber was the radio call sign for the battalion commander who put us in this mess.

"Tell him to come on down and see for himself! Where is he?"

"He's up in the command chopper! Over!"

I squeezed off another burst. Now I knew why the gooks were shooting so high. They weren't shooting at us. They were hitting the massed troops in the landing zone. Good for us, bad for them.

"Well Christ, he's up there! What the fuck does he see?"

"Radio protocol, One-One!"

My world was wracked with insanity. The commander is high over the battlefield and has a God's eye view of the battle. We're pinned down on the ground and can't even lift our heads and *he* wants the update.

And my captain is worried about my radio protocol.

What the fuck? Over.

"Six, where's the support we were supposed to have?" I yelled. "I ain't heard no choppers and there ain't any artillery firing into that jungle!"

"Gunships are inbound, one-one. Do you have smoke? You'll need it to mark your position!"

"Just what the fuck do I have to mark my position for?" I yelled. "The gooks are in the trees. The friendlies have their ass in the grass! And tell the birds about the .51 cal for God's sake! Over!"

I wondered just what the fuck am I bothering with this bullshit for and threw the handset back to the radioman.

"You talk to these assholes! Tell them I'm a little busy."

I grabbed the ammo can next to the radioman and crawled off, choking and sweating and dragging the machine gun. The heat was ungodly. It laid on me like a weight. Breathing was hard but breathing in hot air didn't help. I made it about ten meters and set up. I was now to the right of where the twerp opened fire. I thought that might give me a better vantage point. I opened the bipods and that gave the gun some needed elevation and my arms some needed rest. The shooting seemed to have lessened so I took a chance and raised my head a bit just in time to see why the shooting had slowed. The NVA were coming.

They were moving out of the trees slowly, in a wide line about three hundred meters from me. But they were moving in a line that would take them right into my squad. That couldn't happen. I had wounded down and the rest of the guys couldn't handle the numbers coming at them. I moved forward, inching along so as not to attract any attention. I wanted to get into a bit of a flanking position before I opened up. I had no idea what would happen when I did, but I couldn't think beyond the next few seconds when it would be up to me to save the squad. I opened the ammo can, got the belted rounds connected to the belt already in the gun, and I waited. But I didn't wait long. The gooks were about a hundred meters from their tree line and less than a hundred meters from me when I opened up. I fired off about ten rounds and watched the targets go down. I fired again and more men dropped. I fired a third time and a fourth, knocking down more NVA with each burst. That broke the beginning of their charge and sent them running back into the trees. I squeezed off a couple of long bursts and dropped a few more as they ran. Now it was time to get the hell out of here before they figured out where I was.

I yelled back to the other guys.

"Can you guys make a break for it back to the landing zone?"

"That's affirmative, Sarge. We got the gunner patched

up so he can run a little."

"Give me five seconds to move a little bit and then take off. I'll cover you. Grenadier, you shoot just before you're going to run!"

I moved a little more, but each move was getting harder. The dust, the heat, the exertion, the sweat, they were all sapping my strength with each movement. I set up to fire and heard the thump of the grenade launcher. The guys were making their break so I opened with a long volley spraying across the front of the trees, hoping it would be enough to get the guys back to the relative safety of the landing zone. I ran through a belt of about a hundred rounds and saw something I'd never seen before. The heat of the machine gun barrel started the grass that was touching it on fire.

Wow, that's some dry shit, I thought. Then I heard the best sound of the day. It was the *swoosh-bang* of the rockets fired from our gunships. They crashed into the jungle with explosions of bamboo and dirt, and I hoped, body parts. But I didn't stick around to see. As long as the gunships were making runs, I grabbed as much ammo as I could carry and hoisted the gun over my shoulder and took off running. I could hear the rocket impacts and the drone of the mini-guns that raked the NVA positions but I never stopped running. When I approached the landing zone, I was shocked. Dead and wounded lay all around the clearing.

Medics were working on some and bloody bandages were all over the place. The NVA barrage had played hell with the guys in the LZ even as I thought we were the unlucky ones stranded out in the tall grass. I checked on my squad and found they'd all made it back except the twerp. He wasn't going anywhere. I saw the lieutenant.

"What's the plan, LT?" I asked

"We've got to set up some defense on this side of the LZ," he said. "That machine gun working?"

"Hell, yeah," I said. "The gunner got hit but the gun works just fine."

"Can you find a good spot out there to set up?"

"I passed a big-assed anthill out there about twenty-five meters," I said. "Give me a couple guys and we'll make a stand out there."

"Roger that," he said and pointed to different guys. "You, you, you and you – you're with Duffy. Grab all the ammo laying around."

"I need a couple of thumpers too," I said, and my guy didn't hesitate. The grenade launchers could act as mini-mortars when the assault started. My guy grabbed another grenadier from another platoon.

"He's in too, Sarge," he said, although the other guy didn't look too happy about it.

"When the gunships make their next pass, we head

out to the anthill," I said. "I'll put the gun on the hill and you guys spread out on either side. Grab all the ammo you can find, especially you grenadiers."

We watched as three gunships came whipping out of the south and swept across the jungle, blowing the shit out of everything and everyone.

"Now!" I yelled, and we made a dash for the anthill. We got there just in time to see one of the gunships burst into a yellow and red fireball before crashing in the grass.

Fuck me, I thought, hoping someone thought to warn the pilots about the heavy machine gun.

I popped down behind the anthill, immediately thankful there weren't any ants. I was also thankful the hill wasn't even a few meters farther. I don't think I could have made it. I was heaving now, not breathing. Air came in big gulps instead of breaths. It was hot and dusty and stinking from the constant stream of firing and the sun was stabbing my eyes. On the plus side, I was still able to breathe it.

Shooting down the chopper must have given the gooks a boost of testosterone. The remains of the bird were still flaming when it looked like half of Hanoi came charging out of the jungle, yelling and screaming.

"They've got a long way to run," I told my guys to steady them. "By the time they get close they are going to be exhausted. Be patient and wait till they're close enough for one shot, one kill."

They didn't look too bad, my guys. They were probably scared. If they weren't they were probably insane. But they were holding it together even though none of us had ever been this deep in shit before. As I watched gooks continue their charge I saw something strange. It looked like the fire was charging right behind them. I blinked a couple of times to be sure of what I was seeing and sure enough, the fire was advancing almost as fast as the NVA. The chopper crash ignited the dry grass and what little wind there was carried it in our direction. But the gooks were our biggest worry. They were within a hundred and fifty meters and slowing. They were spent from running and were as exhausted as I had been. They closed another fifty or so meters and I opened up with the hog -- five to ten round bursts, sweeping from right to left and then from left to right. They were falling as fast as I could shoot, but I had to slow down when I saw the barrel of the gun start to heat up again. We'd thought about ammo but not about a second barrel to replace this one if it overheated. On both sides of me the guys were firing. The grenadiers were pumping rounds into the second line advancing on us. The guys in the LZ were taking care of the flanks and I was starting to feel a little more confident. That was premature.

I squeezed off another dozen rounds and paused to let

the barrel cool again when my world exploded. The blast blew me backwards and the gun, or what was left of it, smacked me in the eye. I couldn't see and thought I might have been blinded but someone poured water over my eyes and washed all the dirt and shit out them. I was still hurting but I could at least see.

"What the fuck was that?" I asked, when I got my wits about me.

"RPG, Sarge," the grenadier said. "I saw him lining you up for the shot but I couldn't fire in time." The gook had a rocket propelled grenade launcher and took a shot that blew up the anthill but left me surprisingly in tact.

"Well, fuck," I said, "did you at least have the decency to kill the bastard?"

"We all did, I think," he responded. "He got lit up pretty good from a bee hive round and some M-16 fire."

From behind me, I heard a familiar voice yelling at me.

"Why ain't that gun firing, Duffy?"

I went back to the hill and saw the barrel of the gun sheared right off the receiver.

"Defective barrel, big man!" I yelled back.

'Defective gunner more likely!"

I picked up an M-16 laying close by and started shooting. The NVA charge was stalled in the tall grass and they had a choice to make. The grassfire behind them had blown into a huge curtain of fire. The GIs in front of them had been battered but not beaten. We were still fighting back. I figured they would take their chances with us.

"Big John! Start throwing some M-79 fire on these motherfuckers! They are laying in the grass about seven-five meters in front of me."

"That's a rog!" he yelled back, and immediately I heard the thumping of a couple of launchers.

I turned my attention back to my guys.

"Get ready, men! These fuckers are getting ready to charge again!"

I saw the guys start gathering up ammo and shoring up their game faces. It took about five minutes for the second charge. We were doing OK but without the machine gun, we were being overwhelmed. There were just too many gooks and not enough rifles. Some of the bad guys were getting too close for my comfort but I kept shooting. I didn't have to aim. There were so many of them every shot hit someone.

It was looking pretty bleak when I felt the rounds cracking over my head and the demon screams of someone on a mission. Holcomb plopped down beside me behind the hill and he had a new M-60. I took it from him and propped it up on the hill and started squeezing. I got some but I couldn't get them all. Three NVA came breaking through our position. One guy was so close, I stuck out my leg and tripped him. He responded by shooting me in the leg. I answered by clubbing him in the face with the machine gun. Then one of my guys shot him and ended that contest. The rest of the company was being challenged all up and down the edges of the LZ but were holding. We'd broken the charge and the NVA retreated to regroup and, no doubt, try again. We should have regrouped as well but we were running out of soldiers to regroup. The helicopter rockets had come down in a steady torrent of fire and started more fires on the ground. The flames ate the tall grass and didn't spare the wounded on either side. The temperature on the ground was unbearable. From a hundred yards away, it was still hot enough to make me turn my face away.

I caught a glimpse of the captain in between his radio conversations.

"Hey Six, isn't it about time for reinforcements you talked about yesterday?"

I thought it was an innocent question but the captain glared at me with a look like Superman trying to use his x-ray vision.

"They can't bring them in because of the fires," he said. "There is no place for them to land."

Could this day get any fucking worse? I thought.

The doc came over and patched up my leg. The bullet had grazed me along the shin but hadn't broken any bone. It resulted in a long, nasty cut but I could live with that – I hoped.

Things had gone quiet, at least for the moment. Every now and then, though, a single shot would ring out over on the north side of the LZ.

The big man looked at me and we came to the same conclusion.

"Sniper!"

"Help me over there, Big John. We got to put an end to that shit."

"Roger that, asshole. How did you get yourself shot anyway?"

"Just one of those days, I guess," I said, and we started low crawling toward the north. The fire had ripped through these positions and the guys were sitting ducks. The grass had been their only concealment and now this side of the LZ looked like it was covered in blacktop. We found the third squad leader hunkered down behind the body of one of his dead soldiers. It was that kind of day.

"What have you got?" I asked him.

"There's a fucking sniper popping anything that moves," he said. "If everyone lays still, he's quiet. As soon as someone moves, he opens up."

"Is he hitting anything?" the big man asked.

"Hell, yeah!" the squad leader replied. "He's had four head shots so far."

"Do you know where he is?" I asked.

"We think he's in a tree out to the northeast about two hundred meters out."

Headshots at two hundred meters, I thought. This guy can shoot.

Holcomb looked at me and told me I could take care of this. He wanted to get back in case the NVA launched another assault. I was OK with that. He was more mobile than I and I did think I could handle the sniper. The big man crawled off and I thought of a plan.

"Any grenadiers left?" I asked the third squad leader.

"No, they're both down. I have their weapons though."

"How much closer can I get without drawing a shot?" I asked.

"Not very far," he said. "About ten or fifteen meters and then you're in his sights."

"Do you know how to use the grenade launcher?" I said.

"Yeah, I'm not bad. What do you have in mind?"

"I'm going to low-crawl over to that pile of c-rations over there. You keep an eye on that tree and if he opens up smoke him with a grenade."

"You're fucking crazy. That guy can shoot. You'll never make it."

"Hey Sarge, you have one guy pinning down the whole north side of the LZ. If we take this guy out, your able-bodied guys can stop hiding over here and get over to the east side to help repel the next assault we know is coming."

Before he could say anything else, I started crawling, making sure my helmet was fastened under my chin. If this guy was going for headshots I'll need even this flimsy fucking pot, I thought. I yelled back as I crawled:

"Keep watching the tree and get him with your first shot!"

I don't know what, if anything, he said and I didn't really give a shit. We needed to get this guy. My leg was sore and I knew crawling in the dirt wasn't the best thing for it but it was a war, after all, and you don't get to call timeout for a sub. The c-ration boxes were about ten meters away and I was thinking this was a mistake. My leg felt like the grassfire was burning inside it and I was way past the normal limits of my endurance. But I kept dragging myself through the dust and the heat and then I thought my leg exploded.

I heard the shot after it whacked into my calf. If this

guy was going for headshots, maybe he wasn't as good as advertised. I kept waiting to hear the grenade launcher but nothing happened. I started crawling again and a bullet kicked up the dust a foot from my head.

Maybe he's not so bad after all.

I didn't have the chance to think too much about it. The squad leader popped a grenade into the trees in the distance and no one was shooting at me.

I heard someone shout: "You got the fucker, Sarge!" That let me breathe a little easier.

The third squad's medic was down so somebody else threw a bandage on my new wound and pulled it tight. He stuck me with a hit of morphine too. He told me that was the only way I could deal with the pain and still fight. I told the guys who could still walk to try to get over to the east side of the landing zone to hold off the next assault. They looked at me like I was joking. I looked over at the vulnerable side of the LZ and saw the guys in various stages of relaxation.

What the fuck? I wondered. I had some guys help me get back to what was left of my squad.

"Fellas, did anyone mention that there is a fucking war to fight?" I said.

"Sarge, the Six told us the choppers saw the gooks heading south, away from the LZ," the radioman said. "They think the gooks are bugging out."

That didn't make any sense, I thought. They have as many, if not more, men. They have a shitload of weapons. The fire destroyed a lot of our equipment.

That's it, I thought. The smoke from the fire was covering their movements and if they were moving to the south, they weren't bugging out. They were trying to bug in. They were going to use the gully to come up on us from the south. I saw Big John and waved him over.

"What's with you, Duffy? You like getting shot?"

"Not really but we're all going to get shot if we don't get some men to guard the gully. The gooks are moving south. If they were moving away they'd be heading east. South is where I saw a pretty deep gully that ran from the tree line all the way to ass end of the LZ. That's where they're headed. They are going to jump us from the south."

"Shit,' he said, "there isn't anyone over there. I brought them all up here to defend this side. Everyone who can walk! Get on your feet and follow me. This ain't over yet."

The big man huddled briefly with our lieutenant and continued on to the south end of the LZ.

The lieutenant came over to me.

"We've got fast movers on the way, Duff. They will be able to keep some heads down."

"Yeah, where the fuck were they when we were under

attack? I just hope they get here in time."

"About that, do you really think they will come up the gully?"

My answer was a huge volume of fire roaring out of the south.

"We better hope that the big man can handle that," I said, wanting more than anything to be on the side of that gully ripping up some NVA.

"I'm taking some of the lightly wounded over there to reinforce," LT said. "Can you hold here with these guys?"

"These guys" were all hit and patched up and bloody but they looked lucid enough.

"Can you guys fight?" I asked them.

"Fuck yeah we can fight, Sarge. Just let them come," a little guy said. He looked like he couldn't drink legally in most states but he was a fuck of a soldier.

I arranged them in a rough line of defense. We had two hogs so instead of putting them in the middle where I'd got my face blown to shit, I put them out near the flanks, hoping that if Mr. Charles came at us from the east, we'd get them in a cross fire. And come they did.

We must have battered the gooks pretty good. The gunships and the fires and our resistance definitely messed with their timing. The attack on our side of the perimeter should have been a diversion for the main thrust up the gully but the timing was way off. The battle in the gully had been raging for almost five minutes before the assault from the east came. They hit us hard and for a time I thought they might break through. We were taking a lot of casualties, but we were holding even as the NVA charges kept coming. I turned around to get on the horn to ask about the jets when my radioman's head just exploded in a shower of red. Something hit me near the eye and snapped my head back. That eye was already swollen shut from the explosion of the anthill and now something else hit it.

This bad day got worse. My radioman had been dragging his ass along behind me over every inch of this shitty day. He never balked. He rarely complained. He was just there, the way he was supposed to be. Now the poor fuck is dead. This day better be over soon, I thought. My eyes were a bleeding mess but that couldn't stop me from weeping at the death of this great kid.

The placement of the machine guns worked. We did get them in a real heavy crossfire and that broke the assault just about the time the jets arrived on station. They got the gooks in the open and torched them with napalm. There was still a lot of shooting over in the gully, but I didn't see any gooks charge into the perimeter and that was good.

Five minutes later, our guys were pulling out of the gully. A few minutes later, a jet screamed down dropped a five hundred pounder in the ditch. A minute later, another fast mover dropped a napalm canister that boiled the gully in orange and black flame.

And that was that.

The morphine wore off way too fast and I was a hurting kangaroo. My head was killing me from the battering it had taken. My left eye was swelling and I couldn't see out of my right. Several parts of my arms and legs had been singed by the grassfire and I know my lungs were covered in soot, ash, and dust. Other than that and two gunshot wounds, I was OK.

When the captain came over, he didn't look like someone who just won a battle.

"What's the count?" I asked.

"Everyone," he whispered. "Everyone."

"What do you mean 'everyone?"

"Everyone in the company was killed or wounded," he said. "We don't have a company anymore. We had one hundred and twenty-two at the start. Now, we've got at least sixty-five dead and everyone else wounded."

"Where are you hit, Six?" I asked, and he lifted his shirt. Two bloody bandages covered something I couldn't and didn't want to see.

"Jesus, I knew it was bad but I didn't think it was that bad," I said. "You better sit your ass down before you fall."

With that, I helped him down to rest his back against some mortar ammo crates.

"You seen Big John, Six?"

"That's what I came over to tell you. He died in the gully. He got hit a couple of times but wouldn't go down. He died trying to throw back a gook grenade. He did it twice before the third one blew up in his face.

"I'm sorry, Duffy. I know you two were close."

"Yeah, we were close, captain."

The medevac choppers had landed and started taking out the more seriously wounded. A medic from one of the birds looked at me.

"Aren't you a sight?" he said.

"Watch it, doc, I can still kick your ass."

He wasn't sure if I was joking and neither was I. So he started looking me over.

"What's this?" he said, poking around my battered eye. He pulled some kind of instrument from his kit. "Hold still. I've got to get this out."

He gave it a little yank and held it up to look at it.

"This looks like a piece of bone," he said. "Could it be that's what it is?"

"Yeah, doc. That's about all that's left of my squad."

I know he didn't know what I was talking about.

I looked around the LZ at all the carnage: bloody

shirts and pants, bodies lying with their faces covered, blood everywhere. The fires smoldering and stinking with the flesh they had burned. And that was just our side. How many of the other guys were down? How many fried by the napalm or the grassfires? How many did we shoot? And for what, because some asshole thought he could make his bones as a combat commander?

That's not good enough for me. I've got to get outta this place.

EPILOGUE

They say time heals all wounds. For me, it was the army doctors who told me I'd never walk again without a limp. They said I had some nerve damage in my leg from the bullet wounds. I bet them a case of beer that if they knew their shit, I'd walk as good as new. It took awhile, but after a couple of surgeries and some great physical therapists, I was walking pretty well, well enough that after a couple of extra months in the army, I was discharged. That took care of the physical wounds. More beer and more than a little whiskey were trying to take care of the psychological wounds. I was home again, but it didn't feel like home. A lot of my friends had finished college and moved to big cities like New York or Philly. They moved because they had jobs. I stayed home because I didn't. In fact, I didn't have much. But I knew where the bars were and I had a little route I covered to make sure that they all enjoyed the benefit of my money and when I got drunk, my misery.

I decided to try night school to finish my degree and stay out of those bars. I liked to read and I could diagram a sentence so I thought English might be my forte. I went to the college to register and noticed a very lonely guy sitting at a desk in the far corner of the gym. He had a spiffy uniform on that identified him as a staff sergeant in the good old U.S. Army. I felt kind of bad for him. There wasn't anyone within twenty feet of him except a few assholes who thought it would be manly to throw a few insults his way. He just smiled but I knew that inside, he wanted to chew those pisspots up and spit them out. When I walked by him, I gave him a half-assed salute and a smile. He smiled back.

The first class I registered for was Creative Writing. It was required for my major and I figured I could sling yarns with the best of them. At our first class, the professor gave us a writing assignment to see what our different styles were. I immediately started in with a version of the whorehouse encounter I'd had in Vietnam. I edited a little and erased a lot and finally came up with a version I thought made sense. I handed it in, anxious to hear what the prof had to say about my story. I thought it was pretty good.

We were due to get the papers back at the next class

so I was kind of excited about hearing if my story registered at all. And it certainly did register.

"I didn't grade these papers," the professor started out, "because this was more of a 'get acquainted' exercise. I wanted to gauge the talent level in this class. So I made some remarks on the papers but didn't assign a letter grade."

I thought that was reasonable but I still wanted to hear what he had to say about my story.

The professor went on.

"Is Mr. Duffy here this evening?" he asked.

I raised my hand and he acknowledged me with a shit-eating grin.

"Would you please come up here for a moment?"

I thought this was probably good news. Like I said, I can spin bullshit with the best of them.

The professor addressed the class with his hand on my shoulder.

"It seems that Mr. Duffy here comes to us from across the sea," he said. "Is that correct?"

"Yep," I said. "I've been home from Vietnam for about a month."

"Yes, I surmised that from your story," he said, then turned again to the class. "It seems that Mr. Duffy is so proud of sexually violating a young Vietnamese girl that he used his escapade as the basis for his story."

Violating? She fucking violated me, I thought. What the fuck is this guy trying to do?

A few groans and a lot of pissed-off stares from the women in the class followed.

"Mr. Duffy," the professor said, "I want to render some advice and I truly hope that you heed it.

"That advice is that you resign from this class at your earliest convenience. We are still within the full refund period, so you can still get your money back. I make that recommendation with the promise that should you not resign, I will definitely scar your transcript with an F.

"Under no circumstances will ever give a passing grade to anyone too stupid to avoid service in that immoral war in Vietnam. And your paper illustrates the wisdom of my position."

I was stunned. I stood there, my face getting redder by the minute, this asshole's hand still on my shoulder. My first impulse was to smash his fucking face in and I came really close to doing just that. But I fought the impulse and tried to gather my composure. When I was back in control, I merely brushed the professor's hand off my shoulder and said, much louder than I should have:

"Fuck you, very much, professor."

I snatched my paper from his hand and headed toward the door.

Kiss my fucking ass, I thought. This is what I get? Then I headed to the closest bar.

I was swilling down a shot of Corby's wondering what kind of country I was living in. I get booted from one school because I wasn't military enough and I get booted from a college course because I was military at all.

The next day I went to see the dean about my situation. I explained what had transpired and he shook his head sadly.

"Don't worry a bit, Mr. Duffy," he said. "I'm sure we can get you into another creative writing section in the same time period. You won't miss but a single class."

That was the least of my worries.

"What about the asshole who threatened me in front of twenty or so other students?" I asked. "What about him?"

"Mr. Duffy, it is a sad state of affairs but the asshole, as you so correctly point out, is among the majority now in charge of this institution."

"Wow," I answered. "Here too, huh?"

Here we go again.

-end-

ACKNOWLEDGMENTS

This book would not have been possible without the caring, concerned, and committed counseling I received from the Buffalo VA Medical Center at the hands of retired MSW Barbara Wolfrum and current counselor Monica Jensen. Thank you both for all you've done for me and for all the vets under your care.

Special thanks are owed to my longtime friend and editor Mike Del Nagro whose editing talent is part of every page in the book.

The name John Holcomb appears near the end of my story. He is not a figment of my imagination but rather a true American hero. He perished on 3Dec68 but not before his heroism saved my life at the cost of his own. His reward was a posthumous Medal of Honor while mine was to grow old and bald in the glow of my love for my family. Furthermore, this effort has been an attempt to honor his sacrifice and the sacrifice of so many on that bloody day.

I also thank my friends who survived that awful day: Jim "Mo" Maloney, Ron Balzer, Dave Neamon, Lee Craig, and Lieutenant Larry Gerstner.

Thanks also accrue to the late Mick McCann who flew

helicopters for Charlie Company, 229th Aviation Battalion who provided me with important facts that made great fiction and to Matthew Brennan who wrote "Hunter Killer Squadron," which also gave me better insight into the scout mission in Vietnam.

I also thank Lieutenant Donald Becker, Lieutenant Joe Brett and Tom Donohue for their service and their friendship over these many years.

There really is a Josh Duffy and he is a friend and fellow Vietnam vet but he probably didn't do any of the things described in this book. He has made his own legacy as a Vietnam veteran and as a loyal friend for more than half a century and a fitting model for my hero.

ABOUT THE AUTHOR

Steve Banko served 16 months in combat in Vietnam where he was wounded six times. His awards for heroism included the Silver Star, the nation's third highest decoration for valor, and four Purple Hearts.

Steve spent more than two decades as a speechwriter and professional communicator. He has also spoken to audiences across the country on the issues of war and peace. His non-fiction work has been included in several anthologies and periodicals. This is his first novel.

His speech focusing on post-traumatic stress among combat veterans received the Grand Prize Award from the Cicero Foundation for the best speech of 2010.

Steve lives with his wife, Shirley, in South Buffalo NY and North Ft. Myers Fl.

Made in the USA
Charleston, SC
29 December 2016